To Ryla
Warmest regards
Gower Leconfield

The Prince Must Die

Gower Leconfield*

*Gower Leconfield is the pen name of a prominent
Cambridge-educated international lawyer.*

A Dandelion Books Publication
www.dandelionbooks.net

Tempe, Arizona

P9-CDO-672

Copyright, 2003 by Gower Leconfield

All rights exclusively reserved. No part of this book may be reproduced or trans-lated into any language or utilized in any form or by any means, electronic or mechanical, including photocopying, recording or by any information storage and retrieval system, without permission in writing from the publisher.

Published Worldwide
by Dandelion Books, Tempe, Arizona

A Dandelion Books Publication
Dandelion Enterprises, Inc., Tempe, Arizona

Library of Congress Cataloging-in-Publication Data

Leconfield, Gower
    The prince must die

Library of Congress Catalog Card Number 2002113479
ISBN 1-893302-72-5

Book covers and interior design by Jonathan Gullery

Disclaimer and Reader Agreement

Under no circumstances will the publisher, Dandelion Books, LLC, or author be liable to any person or business entity for any direct, indirect, special, inci-dental, consequential, or other damages based on any use of this book or any other source to which it refers, including, without limitation, any lost profits, business interruption, or loss of programs or information.

Reader Agreement for Accessing This Book

By reading this book, you, the reader, consent to bear sole responsibility for your own decisions to use or read any of this book's material. Dandelion Books, LLC and the author shall not be liable for any damages or costs of any type arising out of any action taken by you or others based upon reliance on any materials in this book.

Printed in the United States of America

Dandelion Books (logo)
www.dandelionbooks.net

For all my friends at Cambridge

Tell them in England, if they ask
What brought us to these wars,
To this plateau beneath the night's
Grave manifold of stars—
It was not fraud or foolishness,
Glory, revenge or pay:
We came because our open eyes
Could see no other way.

— *Cecil Day Lewis*

Prologue

LONDON — Prince Charles spent the night in the hospital after he took a tumble off his horse yesterday while playing polo and briefly lost consciousness.

The 52-year-old heir to the British throne was playing on a team at a charity match in Cirencester with his sons William and Harry when he fell awkwardly, but did not break any bones, his office said.

The prince regained consciousness very quickly and was taken to Cirencester Hospital by ambulance as a precautionary measure, his office said.

He was later transferred to Cheltenham Hospital for an overnight stay.

—*Post Wire Services*

Part One

Chapter One

Cambridge, April, 2001. It was night. Sir Adrian Waterloo raised his glass and glanced around at those seated at the table in the dining room on the top floor of the Pitt Club, one of the last bastions of High Toryism. All in evening dress, they were flushed with fine claret and satiated with seven exquisite courses. The candles glittered in the otherwise dark room.

"Gentlemen, the Queen."

They all rose.

"The Queen," they responded in unison.

After they had concluded the toast, a rotund, red-faced man with a mane of grey hair stood up and lifted his glass:

"But not Prince Charles."

There was a moment of intense silence, broken by some muttering. Finally, they all rose again.

"But not Prince Charles," they repeated, draining their glasses.

After the anti-toast, the grey-haired man continued:

"Do you know what the bloody Frogs have done?"

Sir Adrian chuckled:

"What now, Professor Lamont-Hope? What new obscenities?"

"Monkeys. They've got wild monkeys in the parks. In Paris. In the Bois de Boulogne. They got them as pets, but when they got big, they stopped being cute, so they released them in the park. The bloody monkeys come down from the trees and attack people. They go right for the men's nuts. You see the point?"

"Point? No, not really. Typical French nonsense, but what else?"

"Look around in St. James's Park and don't tell me you don't see monkeys."

"You mean ...?"

"Of course. The bloody wogs. The immigrants, the Pakis, the West Indians, the lot of them. And the fags. They are our fucking monkeys and don't think they're not going for our nuts."

"Bloody Prince Charles," Sir Adrian snorted. "He's all for them."

"Precisely the point. The land of hope and glory is going down the tubes like the rest of Europe. Nottingham is all black. Not a white face anywhere. And Tony Blair just signs them up for Labor. His entire cabinet is fag. He couldn't care less."

The dinner guests were becoming agitated, waving their cigars and gulping their port. Liveried waiters rushed around refilling their glasses.

"Bloody wogs, bloody wogs, get them out! Ban the fags!" a chorus began chanting, as they pounded their fists on the table.

"Well, this is the St. George Association," Sir Adrian offered, "and St. George did slay the dragon."

"Slay the dragon!" Lamont-Hope nodded. "Slay the fucking dragon."

"Hear, hear!" the rest shouted.

"But how?" Sir Adrian pondered.

"Where there's a will, there's a way," Lamont-Hope snapped.

A strange-looking, pale and emaciated codger of about eighty with a beaked nose and in full evening dress, including winged collar, rose uneasily, holding his silver-tipped cane tightly. He held up his glass, his hand quivering.

"To St. George and Prince William!"

There was a moment of silent concurrence. They all rose, holding up their glasses.

"St. George and Prince William."

The codger sneered.

"Not that fag, Edward."

"Which one is worse, Charles or Edward?" Sir Adrian pondered.

"Charles," they shouted.

"Kill the head and the body dies," Lamont-Hope challenged. "Clear out the lot, including the witch Camilla. Except for William. Get rid of Charles, force the Queen to abdicate, and we've got a clean slate. Gentlemen, we must sing 'Jerusalem.'"

They sang. After the last verse, a waiter, who had been standing directly behind the old man, said:

"Viscount Harrington, none of you has been discreet. But be assured that we are with you. We are Middle Britain."

The dinner ended in a haze of cigar smoke and they left. Out on the street, Viscount Harrington, Professor Lamont-Hope and Sir Adrian Waterloo congregated briefly.

"He'll be in a polo match outside Newmarket," Viscount Harrington explained. "He can fall off his horse and break his neck. We use the same vet. I'll take care of it."

"What if he doesn't die?" Sir Adrian asked.

"If you don't succeed at first, try, try again," Lamont-Hope offered.

"Very well, then," Viscount Harrington said. "I'll give it a shot."

"Are you certain you can trust the vet?" Sir Adrian asked.

"I pay him enough," Harrington retorted. "Besides, he deals drugs on the side. He knows I know. Not a sticky wicket by a long shot. Get going, get going, or we might get rounded up."

"Can't have that," Sir Adrian nodded.

"Conspiracy to kill Prince Charles uncovered outside the Pitt Club," Lamont-Hope grinned.

"No joking matter," Harrington coughed, "the future of Britain is at stake. We all know Diana was murdered. There are other forces to contend with. The republicans want to knock off all the royals, put in a new Cromwell. They'll stop at nothing. No time to lose."

"When's Newmarket?" Sir Adrian asked.

"In a week's time. Got to get cracking." Harrington stumbled toward his Bentley. "Even this bloody car is no longer a British jewel," he lamented. "The Krauts grabbed it. Beat them in two wars and it's as though they defeated us. Fuck the lot of them!"

Harrington waved his cane in a fury and got into the Bentley.

"That man is mad," Sir Adrian said.

"We are all mad," Lamont-Hope countered. "Goodnight."

"To Newmarket, then."

"To Newmarket. Indeed."

Chapter Two

The weather cleared somewhat at Newmarket. The Argentinean contingent was resplendent, a huge repast of grilled meats spread out, buffet-style, dark men and women in snazzy clothes lounging in anticipation of the match. Camilla, dressed in a tweed skirt and tan cashmere sweater, mingled casually among them, sipping a Pimms Cup. In an instant, the opposing sides went at it in a fury, the glistening ponies charging as the men in helmets, their muscular bare arms bulging, whacked away at the ball with their mallets. The diffident, dorky Charles was transformed into a handsome, fearless warrior, like a medieval English king leading his men into battle.

"That's the problem with royalty," a handsome Argentinean joked. "They can't be violent in the real world. To be authentic royalty, you have to be feared. This is only polo, only a game. The real players are not the royals. They are only pawns."

A dark beauty smiled:

"Except Arab royalty. Arab royalty has power."

"Which is why they will be destroyed. By their own people or by the Americans."

Suddenly there was a commotion on the field.

"God," Camilla screamed. "It's Charles. He's down. His horse is on top of him."

Everyone stood up and rushed to the edge of the field. Camilla was frantic. She ran towards the fallen polo pony, which was bellowing in pain and kicking its legs violently. The inert body of Prince Charles lay underneath it.

"Call an ambulance, get a doctor," she shouted. "Do something."

Trainers ran out onto the field and attempted to lift the horse and extricate Charles, without success. Blaring sirens became louder as the ambulance and police cars raced to the scene. A truck with a forklift pulled up adjacent to the fallen animal. The driver maneuvered the jaws directly over the body, fastened them and hoisted it, then moving it several yards away from the prostrate prince, let it drop with a thud. Armed police from the Metropolitan Police Services quickly surrounded the Prince of Wales, as several doctors began examining him. They lifted him gingerly, put him on a stretcher and carried him to the ambulance, which tore off with Camilla in it, the MPS screaming along with it.

"Obviously a stress fracture," a painfully thin vet exclaimed, after poring over the carcass. "It's still alive, but barely."

He removed a revolver from his pocket, aimed it at the horse's head and fired. It quivered and then lay still. It was dead.

"Scoop it up," the vet ordered. "We must do a full examination. Take it to my facility."

"Dr. Rogerson? You are Dr. Michael Rogerson?" a ruddy-faced and corpulent plainclothes detective asked.

"Yes. That's right."

"You're Viscount 'Arrington's vet, isn't that right?"

"Yes. Why do you ask?"

"I love the races, sir. I follow Viscount 'Arrington's horses. I read everything about 'em. His trainers, his vet, the lot. Here's hoping His Royal Highness will survive. What with all the problems the royals been havin', they don't need another bloody accidental death."

"Quite right," Rogerson snapped briskly and walked away.

"But if you don't mind, we'll want a full report. I'm Detective Inspector Stanley West, Cambridge police."

Rogerson turned and waited for him to approach. West handed him his card, which Rogerson took perfunctorily.

Paparazzi surrounded the Cambridge hospital in which Charles lay, undergoing surgery. A large crowd of spectators had gathered, straining to see what was going on, a cordon of police keeping them at a distance. A BBC television crew with a stunningly beautiful commentator of Indian extraction had set up shop. She spoke into the camera:

"At this moment," she intoned in a perfect Oxbridge accent, "the reports from the hospital are sketchy. We do know that Camilla is by his side and that the entire royal family is deeply concerned. The Queen is expected momentarily. We are waiting for one of the surgeons to give us an update as soon as that is possible. We do know that Charles is miraculously alive. Beyond that, all is presently conjecture, except that the Prince's office has reported the event as an unfortunate accident. This is Dajit Gupta speaking to you from Cambridge."

David Lamont-Hope sat in his rooms in Great Court, Trinity, watching the BBC broadcast and sipping a large scotch, neat.

"A fuck-up," he hissed to himself. "A bloody, goddamned fuck-up. Harrington is a fucking fool. Did he really think he could pull this off?"

The phone rang. It was Sir Adrian Waterloo.

"What now?" he asked.

"Not over the bloody phone," Lamont-Hope muttered. "Come to my rooms tomorrow for lunch."

He slammed the phone down, sank into his leather chair and sighed.

"What's that word they use in America all the time?" he rambled. "Assholes?"

Sir Adrian arrived promptly at one o'clock and was greeted by Lamont-Hope, who closed the door quickly and filled two sherry glasses with a vintage Manzanilla.

"Bloody jerk survived. I gather he looks like a mummy, wrapped from head to toe with bandages, one leg hoisted up in the air. Harrington's vet better get that report right."

Sir Adrian sniffed his glass and cautiously took a sip.

"Good stuff, David. You always have good stuff."

"An endowed chair helps, Adrian, but this standing on the sidelines is insufferable. Getting rid of Charles probably isn't even enough. We want Portillo in there as prime minister. Blair must go, but Hague is a total jerk."

"I've spoken with Harrington. Discreetly, don't worry. He has a new idea."

"Like what? Dropping a bomb on Buckingham Palace? Having him trampled by a flock of sheep? We don't have bloody forever."

"Don't know, actually. Says we need to go up to his estate in Scotland and work it out."

Lunch was braised sweetbreads washed down with a Nicolas Feuillatte Palmes D'Or, '92, well chilled.

"You drink champagne with lunch every day, David?"

Lamont-Hope gave him a look of ironic intensity.

"I make an effort to do it. At a certain age, life starts to lack meaning unless you do two things: indulge yourself and take risks."

"What do you call what we're doing?"

"Both."

Lamont-Hope reached over with the bottle and refilled Waterloo's glass.

"What will we drink to?" Waterloo asked.

"How about not fucking up?"

"Sounds good to me. But how do we manage it?"

"We get somebody who knows what he's doing."

"Easier said than done, I say."

"In our case, it's got to do with what Shaw said: 'Those who can, do. Those who can't, teach.' You're the Provost of King's College; I'm the University Professor of History. A bit late in the day to become doers, what? But what we can do is get someone who *is* a fucking doer. That's how we won't fuck up. By finding the chap, we *become* doers. 'Easier said than done' is not for doers. It's for bystanders. And I, for one, am not going to die a fucking bystander."

"Harrington is a doer."

"I'll grant you that. But at eighty, he's over the hill. But we'll go up there and hear him out. So, to not fucking up."

He lifted his glass, as did Waterloo.

"To not fucking up," they recited in unison.

"Bloody good lunch," Waterloo smiled.

"This time, the bloody prince is dead."

Waterloo rose silently, shook Lamont-Hope's hand weakly and left.

At the hospital, the police dispersed the crowd as the Queen's shiny black 1978 Phantom VI pulled up. At the tip of the hood, her mascot, a silver replica of St. George on a horse, was poised over a slain dragon.

People were waving Union Jacks and cheering.

"Give 'im our love, Ma'am," a short, plump elderly lady shouted.

The Queen waived benignly at her and was ushered into the hospital.

"Where's Prince Philip?" someone shouted, "Where's Prince Philip?"

"'E's with the abos in Australia," another answered. "Be here tonight."

The Queen entered Charles's room, a white-coated doctor directly behind her. The Prince was conscious, but groggy. Camilla was seated next to his bed, her hand on his bandaged arm.

"Nasty fall," the Queen offered. "Hard luck."

"We'd have killed those grease balls," Charles whispered uneasily.

Camilla let out a roar.

"Just joking," Charles managed. "Great chaps, the Argentineans, really. Don't blame them for being pissed over the Falklands. Where are the boys?"

"William's in Chile. Be back tomorrow." The queen folded and unfolded her hands. "Harry had some exams."

"He shouldn't talk, Ma'am," the doctor said. "But he's doing much better. His leg is broken in three places, two fractured ribs, a bruised kidney and a mild concussion. I would venture that he's had a bit of good luck."

"The food is dreadful," Camilla joked. "Can't you do any better than fin and haddie and bangers and mash? I thought this was 'Cool Britannia,' not 'Chips With Everything!'"

"They're doing their best," the Queen replied calmly.

"Thank you, Ma'am," the doctor bowed sycophantically.

"Cheer up, Charles," said the Queen. "I'll die one day and you'll be king. But you're going to have to be more careful."

"Mother," the Prince remonstrated.

Chapter Three

Asher Gideon was feeling good. He had a few days off from his Mossad duties and was in Paris. He had just successfully executed a leader of Hamas in Geneva without leaving a trace, by shooting him in the face with a gas pistol containing five cc of hydrocyanic acid as he was entering his apartment. Death was attributed to heart failure.

Gideon lived well and dressed well. He liked beautiful women. When his eyes fell on the Swedish blonde at the bar of the Hotel Lautrec on the rue d'Amboise where he was staying, he smiled at her seductively from his table. He was nursing a Pernod and smoking a Gitane. She toasted him with her wineglass, smiled back, and uncrossing her long, deeply tanned legs, languidly poured herself from the bar stool. Her short, tight, sleeveless black dress was deeply cut, exposing a considerable amount of cleavage. She was about five-ten, six feet in her spiked black heels, and moved across the bar like a panther to his table. Gideon rose and gestured for her to sit and join him. She had classic Swedish-blue eyes. Her lips parted as she smiled, revealing brilliant perfect teeth.

"I don't usually accept invitations from strange men, even dark handsome ones," she purred in her Swedish singsong. "Mind if I have one?"

Her smile dazzled him. She sat down opposite him and he offered her the pack of Gitanes. She pulled one out, put it in her sensuous mouth and leaned over for him to light it. She was braless and her breasts were clearly visible. From Gideon's vantage point, they looked stunningly beautiful and inviting. "A perfect ten," he thought to himself.

It wasn't long before they were in his room. She pushed him onto the bed and attacked him, tearing off his clothes, holding his testicles in her hand and gently squeezing. He lay on the bed, moaning in pleasure as she took off her dress. She kept her panties and spiked heels on. She lay on him and kissed him deeply, her left hand pulling his head back by his hair. With her right hand she jabbed the needle that she had concealed in her shoe, into his thigh. He let out a scream. The poison entered his veins rapidly, and in an instant he was dead. She dragged him under the covers to make it look as though he were asleep, kicked off her heels and opened her oversize handbag. She pulled out a running suit, sweat socks and a pair of Nikes, put them on, and pulled off her blonde wig, which she tossed with the spiked heels and the dress into the bag, along with the hypodermic needle.

Looking into the mirror, she wiped off her lipstick, straightened her short, jet-black hair, put on a dark blue watch cap and darted out into the corridor, softly shutting the door behind her. Then she converted the bag into a backpack and slipped it on. Out on the street, she went into her jog in the misty Paris night. After about a mile she took a tiny cell phone from a jacket pocket, stopped and punched in a number.

"It is Ramos. Gideon is dead."

Placing the phone back in her jacket pocket, she resumed running. Then she vanished.

Chapter Four

Viscount Simon Harrington's ancestral estate of over a thousand acres was in a remote corner of Scotland, northeast of Scone. The vast stone castle, overlooking Loch Lynne, was constructed in 1286 and stood majestically on five acres, surrounded by a sheep meadow, game park, gardens, extensive wooded areas and a pond. The long driveway leading up to the castle was lined with tall poplar trees and glorious beds of flowers, including Japanese primrose and sage in full bloom. The cacophony of the rose, purple and white of the primrose was heightened by the bright red and intense blue of the sage.

Daimlers, Jaguars, Vauxhalls, and, incongruously, Range Rovers, drove up majestically to the house. All in all, there were seven cars and a total of twelve men, dressed in tweeds and sporting clothes of various types. Leading them up to the house where a butler in full livery met them, were Sir Adrian Waterloo and Professor Lamont-Hope. Uniformed servants, who had opened the doors to let them out, entered the cars and drove off in them to some unseen destination to park them.

"One is tempted to request a place for five," Sir Adrian joked.

Standing in the huge foyer in front of a gargantuan fireplace, Viscount Harrington, haggard and hawk-like, greeted them in a Scottish plaid kilt and green blazer. The hairy, bony knees of his skinny bowed legs protruded like miniature gargoyles.

Simon Harrington's brusque manner belied a subtle and devious mind capable of the most arcane machinations. His vast wealth was not entirely inherited; he was engaged in various highly profitable enterprises incorporated mostly in the Cayman Islands, the proceeds from which he concealed in his secret accounts in Switzerland and on Grand Cay. He was the owner of Trafalgar Freight, a shipping company incorporated under Nigerian law, which transported child slaves to the cocoa plantations in West Africa. Since his ships flew the Nigerian flag, they were not subject to the labor laws of the western democracies, enabling him to employ African, Asian, and South American seamen at minimal wages and requiring them to work in subhuman conditions. At the same time he was chairman of the board of Radcliffe Chocolates, the world's largest candy manufacturer, which purchased the cocoa. With headquarters in Reading, England, Radcliffe dominated the chocolate business in America through its various subsidiaries that manufactured such popular candy bars as Fudgy Treats and Sweetie Pies. Radcliffe was also the parent company of the popular American fast-food chain, Waldo's, which served cheap hamburgers made of ground meat from cattle raised in Central America on ranches created by leveling the rain forest. Harrington was also a managing director of the Carlyle Group and a confidant of Frank Carlucci.

Like most men of his ilk who engaged in similar nefarious activities in the name of private enterprise, Harrington was unable to see any connection between the manner in which he lived and the suffering he inflicted. Above all, he deemed himself a patriot, whose sole motive was the restoration of British greatness. "Put the 'great' back in Great Britain," was his favorite expression, which he would pronounce at any moment he deemed it appropriate. The absolute last straw for him was losing his vote in the House of Lords as a hereditary peer. "Might as well tear down the statue of Coeur-de-Lion in front of Parliament and just put up a second one of Cromwell," he barked at this indignity.

Harrington's favorite pastime was sponsoring contests of "The Bà," a game peculiar to the Orkney Islands involving two teams of hundreds of players battling to shift a rock-hard ball. He was fond of explaining his passion for "The Bà" by stating perfunctorily, "There are no rules." It was, of course, his philosophy of life. Anxious to be off to the Orkney Islands for a particularly important meeting to keep the sport alive in the face of a threat by the local council to stop paying for the damages caused by the players, he was determined to resolve "this nasty business of Prince Charles," as he referred to it, swiftly and efficiently.

"Let's cut to the chase," he rasped. "We know why we're here. Follow me."

He led them past armored mannequins and portraits of his ancestors, up a magnificent spiral staircase and down a long corridor.

"In here." He pointed to an innocuous-looking door.

Inside was a pristine lecture room with chairs and a podium. The furnishings were simple and functional, the only decoration a large portrait of Alfred the Great behind the podium. Harrington took his place behind the podium and the others took seats, Waterloo and Lamont-Hope directly in front of him.

Harrington reached inside the podium and took out a folder that contained computer printouts.

"Security precautions have obliged me to do a check on all of us, including myself," he said. "Security here is airtight, be assured of that. I have done a clean sweep of the place for bugging devices. Anti-bugging devices are in place. We are the thirteen. We hold the future of Britain in our hands."

"Well," Sir Adrian countered, "it wasn't one of us who fucked up at Newmarket."

"That was close, damned close," Harrington said. "The vet got it right. Bloody horse fell the wrong way."

"A bit much, " Lamont-Hope retorted, "blaming it on the horse."

"What's done is done," Harrington went on. "The report will call it an accident, a fracture. We're in the clear there."

Harrington perceived restlessness in the room.

"Why are we farting around like this?" a lycanthropic individual in a brown tweed suit exclaimed.

"Farting around? What do you mean farting around?" Harrington hissed.

The man was the Duke of Winchester, Morley D'Ascoygne-Gascoygne. Totally hirsute, with wild black hair and beard, he had angry hairs sticking out of his nose and great tufts of hair growing from his ears like shrubs. He had a grey pallor and a strange, dark nose that came to a narrow point at the end. Rising to speak, like a feral beast in the forest, he exclaimed:

"We've all been screened and recruited by you. We all have a common objective and a common motive. Charles is a socialist, that's all there is to it. I personally don't give a bloody damn whom he fucks. He's in cahoots with the reds. Those bastards know how to do it. They'll never have a revolution in Britain. They'll just bleed us to death slowly. With the Cold War over, nobody suspects what they're up to. That's the thing with the lefties in this country. They never fucking give up. The whole point of royalty is that they know what it means to be royalty. If you can't count on them to protect us, what's the point? William knows on which side his bread is buttered. He got that from his mother. He's one of us. And the people love him."

"I can assure you," Harrington responded, "that William knows nothing. But when he's an orphan, the people will love him that much more. He's High Tory to the core. He reeks of it. He knows the difference between noblesse oblige and Leon Trotsky. But Charles and Camilla, they're the most hated couple in the U.K. Charles knows the only way he can survive is by cutting a deal with the left. Labor needs him and he needs Labor, a detestable symbiotic relationship."

"Very well, then," the Duke confided, "I believe I know what we've got to do."

Lamont-Hope grinned.

"I believe there is a consensus."

"I mean, specifically," the Duke said.

"Exactly," Harrington added.

"Lamont-Hope and I have concluded that we need to get the right person to do it," Sir Adrian drawled.

"Les beaux esprits se rencontrent," the Duke puffed in a

dreadful French accent.

"Well," a tall and elegantly thin barrister named Philip Marbury observed, "if our great minds are all working together, who will it be?"

The most prominent criminal defense lawyer in England, Marbury was shrewd and understated. He won acquittals of notorious criminals by quietly and cleverly demolishing the evidence of the prosecution without their ever being aware that he was doing it.

There was a prolonged silence.

"I thought that would be the answer," Marbury chuckled, "so I came prepared."

He did not reveal that he and Harrington had discussed this before the meeting. Harrington was sufficiently clever not to appear to be bullying his point of view through, recognizing that even his gigantic ego was equaled by the egos of his guests. A wily lawyer with a razor-sharp mind, Marbury was the perfect confidant who could guard a secret and conceal his agenda.

"Does the name Heinrich Müller ring a bell?" he asked nonchalantly.

"Head of the Gestapo?" Sir Adrian responded.

"Exactly," Marbury shot back.

Marbury was familiar with the work of E. H. Cookridge, a cloudy figure who wrote a biography of Reinhard Gehlen, the head of Nazi intelligence who had been recruited to the CIA by Allen Dulles after the war. Pulling out a dusty volume of *Gehlen—Spy of the Century,* he read aloud that SS Obergruppenfuhrer Heinrich Müller, known as "Gestapo-Müller," had been an "old Nazi." His radical views and disdainful description of most of the Nazi leaders as "decadent" and "bourgeois" led some in Hitler's inner circle to regard him as a communist at heart rather than a real National Socialist. But no one questioned the Gestapo chief's total loyalty to Hitler, to whom he was devoted. He was always included with Goering, Goebbels, Bormann and Haydrich in their daily visits to Hitler's headquarters. Second in command to Himmler in the SS, Müller was responsible for the investigation that led to the destruction of the notorious "Red Orchestra," the Soviet Union's vast wartime espionage network in Germany. Cookridge speculated that when Müller vanished in 1945, it was almost certain he had defected to the Russians. "Several people claim to have seen him as a Soviet official in East Germany after the war; it is believed that he died in Moscow in 1949," he concluded in a footnote.

Then Marbury produced a recent copy of the *New York Times*, which reported on the release of CIA Nazi files, including Hitler's and Müller's. He read:

"The historians said the files showed that the agency investigated the fate of Müller in 1970 and 1971. Some researchers have said they believe he was killed late in the war or might have survived to collaborate with the Soviet Union. Others thought that he might have been recruited by American intelligence. The files indicate that the CIA reached no conclusion about him."

"All disinformation," Marbury quipped. "Books, newspapers, all contain planted information as part of the inoculation principle. You tell a bit of the truth to conceal a bigger lie. We know Müller was a double agent. American intelligence recruited him to go over to the Soviets to spy on them. When he was found out, British intelligence helped get him out of East Germany under an assumed name and into Switzerland, where he continued to oversee various intelligence and assassination operations for the CIA. He maintained a secret school for assassins, with highly trained, recruited individuals whose sole motive was profit, apart from their predilection for controlled violence. Müller's funeral was practically a state event. The leadership of the school passed to a group of his recruits with no loyalty to anyone, who changed location to avoid detection. It is difficult to contact them, but possible."

Marbury knew all this because of his ties to MI6. It was not exactly true to say his occupation as a criminal defense lawyer was a cover, but he was on personal terms with the head of MI6 and performed operations for them abroad, which were invariably paid for by private companies. The South African giant, Anglo American, funded his numerous trips to South Africa, where he met extensively with the British ambassador, Sir Robin Renwick, and which led to the release of Nelson Mandela from Robin Island on the condition that Mandela turn on his former Communist allies once he took power. It was rumored that Marbury's ability to obtain acquittals or reduced sentences for his infamous clients was mysterious and might in some way be related to a secret source of power he had within the system. He was, in short, a man of many talents.

"Our job is to make contact with that group and find out how much the contract will cost," Marbury concluded.

"Don't know if I like the idea of dealing with a pack of bandits," Montague Rogerson objected. A psychiatrist who specialized in transsexual disorders, he was never quite able to separate his own identity from that of Eton, where he had been captain of the cricket team. He was also Dr. Michael Rogerson's older brother.

Lamont-Hope came to Marbury's defense:

"You've got a better idea?"

Rogerson sat down, shaking his head.

Harrington perked up: "We all trust Marbury to make the contact and find out the cost. No objections? Very well, we stand adjourned."

Chapter Five

Montague Rogerson waited in his office on Eaton Square for the arrival of his new patient, an ostensibly wealthy man who had said over the phone that he was struggling with his sexual identity. He had just come from lunch at The Antelope on Eaton Terrace, one of the last refuges of the old London before it had steadily and relentlessly been turned into a form of Los Angeles.

Traffic poured through Eaton Square now, depriving it of its exclusive elegance and subdued tranquility. Rogerson's address was highly fashionable, and patients preferred this to some nondescript space in a high-rise office building in which confidentiality seemed to be belied by the starkness of the walls and the vast spaciousness of the windows. A psychiatrist required, at least, the illusion of discretion, so he stayed put.

His personal, antique-filled flat was upstairs, his comfortable downstairs office a hodgepodge of chairs, sofas, scattered books and exotic rugs. It was his habit to sit on one sofa while the patient sat on another one, cattycorner to it. On a coffee table he was always careful to put a box of tissues in preparation for the outbursts that invariably came during particularly intense sessions, when, overwhelmed by the power of their own confessionals, patients burst into floods of uncontrolled tears.

Rogerson was a conservative in his profession. It was his conviction that many forms of psychiatric disorders were not caused by chemical imbalances but by the failure of society to impose standards of behavior on people with sufficient power so as to make challenges to them appear to be the very cause of the disorder. Too much freedom, he believed, lay at the heart of psychosexual ambivalence. Freud's *Civilization and Its Discontents* further reinforced his view that it was better to

have some people somewhat discontented than to have civilization destroyed in a miasma of self-absorption. His empha-
sis was on adjustment to the external world, not the alteration
of the self to contradict the given. "The trouble with transsexuals," he would insist, "is that they confuse the organ with
the signifier." The endless analysis of "that screwball Schreber,"
as Rogerson described him, was a colossal waste of time.
"Imagining that God is making love to you or that you are
making love to yourself because you are both man and woman,
is not really interesting," Rogerson would joke. "Much ado
about nothing," he dismissed it. "Man should have taken a
cold bath and been done with it." Yet he was indulgent with
his own patients, not only tolerating their eccentricities, but
actually encouraging them as long as they confined themselves
to the existing social order and engaged in them discreetly.

In spite of profoundly conservative reservations about trans-
sexuality and his utter distaste for the surgical solutions that
had found favor in the profession, he had read enough Robert
Stoller to accept that there were a few authentic cases, but in
his own estimation, very few. In his own practice he had never
counseled "mutilation," as he referred to it, but obliged anyone suffering from what he considered "delusions" about his
sexual identity to undergo extensive analysis to rectify what he
was convinced was a condition brought about by child abuse.

But nothing in his entire career had prepared him for what
now stood before him, a man of such incredible beauty that he
was unable to take his eyes off him even for a second. Christian
von Oberman was about thirty years old with finely chiseled
symmetrical features and soft, straight, light-brown hair that fell
gently on his brow. His nose was perfectly proportioned and his
sensuous lips hinted at a refined yet disdainful arrogance. The
high cheekbones lent something of the Tartar to his otherwise
Aryan allure, undoubtedly the result of some aristocratic Polish
blood. Approximately five-foot ten, he had a body that was lithe
and supple, not at all stiff like a typical German. His pale skin
was almost translucent and his chin had a slight engaging cleft.

His astonishing teeth glistened like rare pearls. But it was his eyes that mesmerized Rogerson. They were deep, intoxicatingly green and unblinking, like those of some strange feline monster lurking in the jungle about to pounce.

Von Oberman was dressed impeccably in a dark blue double-breasted Savile Row suit, pinched at the waist and with double vents, a crisp white shirt with Old Harrovian cuff links, and a regimental claret, black, and gold tie that Rogerson recognized as a Cambridge Hawks Club cravat. He spoke English flawlessly, with a high Oxbridge accent. Only if Rogerson listened carefully, could he detect the slight inflection of Oberman's Teutonic origins.

"Dr. Rogerson," he extended his hand, "I need your help."

Rogerson sank deep into his leather sofa and exhaled. The clutter of his office belied the order of his mind and the precision of his scientific approach, which he had honed over years of intimate relationships with patients and colleagues. He put his fingertips to his lips and remained silent for several seconds.

"Yes, perhaps…"

"Dr. Rogerson, I have an ostensibly perfect life," von Oberman interjected. "I come from a family with enormous resources and prestige. We are Bavarian nobility. In Britain, it is not polite to speak of one's finances, but the fact is that I am rich. I am, actually, a prince. I have had a superb education, mostly in Britain, at Harrow and Magdalene College, Cambridge, where I took degrees in Chemistry and Art History. My work is gratifying. I am with the Courtauld Institute where I head the department of artistic authentication, a position that enables me to employ my scientific and humanities education in a most constructive way, discovering if works of art are what they are believed to be. I am an expert, if you will, in authenticity. And I am engaged to be married to Lady Sarah Filburn, herself an accomplished woman, a graduate of Oxford and a superb cellist. She is utterly beautiful. But I am living a sort of lie, because I am convinced I am an imposter. The expert on authenticity is himself inauthentic."

Rogerson did what he could to assume a mordantly avuncular demeanor, both as a defense mechanism against his own attraction to the prince and as a way of avoiding any hint of sentimentality that might undermine his credibility.

Since the death of his wife, Rogerson suspected he was becoming as dependent on his patients as they were on him. After her death he had sold his house in Kent and moved permanently into town, ensconcing himself in his current digs above his office, "to be closer to my work," he explained to friends. Work and conservative politics absorbed him, as did his social life, which revolved around his membership at White's.

"Freud believed that everyone, even the most successful amongst us, has a sense of being an imposter, of inauthenticity. It's perfectly normal," he said.

"But, in my case, it is more than that. I doubt, very seriously, my authenticity as a man. I dream, almost every night, that I am a woman. And when I make love, I feel that I am the woman, that I am being penetrated, not the other way around."

Rogerson was not unfamiliar with this sort of fantasy. He was neither unsympathetic nor impatient; it was not something he regarded as unusual or dysfunctional.

"Look," he nodded, "all men have a female aspect. It's something that most men deny. Consider yourself lucky that yours is coming out. Do you ever cross-dress? I know a successful surgeon, happily married with four children, who wears women's panties under his trousers when he goes in to operate. Considering his success rate, I told him not to stop."

Von Oberman laughed softly.

"I know of this sort of thing. But I am different. Each day, I find myself identifying more and more with the feminine. It is starting to become overwhelming."

"When you masturbate, how do you do it?"

"That's a presumption you make, doctor, but yes, I do masturbate. When I do, I rub my thighs together. I never touch my penis with my hands. I think of my penis as my enemy, also my genitals. I think I would be perfectly happy without them."

Rogerson typed a few notes on his laptop.

"Excuse me," he apologized. "I don't have perfect recall. We will need to explore this more deeply."

"But, Dr. Rogerson," von Oberman pleaded, "I think I know the answer already. Can you recommend a surgeon?"

"Have you any idea what you would be giving up?" Rogerson half-shouted.

Von Oberman stared at him, suddenly looking vulnerable. He began to cry.

"I can help you," Rogerson told him, handing him the box of tissues. "But I have no quick solution. I need to explore the reality of your inner life. If you wish to work with me, I think you will find that, in the end, this is the best course. But that is up to you."

Von Oberman wiped his eyes.

"You are right. I must do it," he concluded.

"Good," Rogerson smiled. "We can set up a series of appointments. You should come two days a week. What about Mondays and Wednesdays, in the late afternoon, say, four o'clock?"

"Could it be later? My work…"

"Yes, of course. Six?"

"That is much better. I will be here on Monday at six. Thank you."

Rogerson got up and escorted him to the door. They shook hands warmly and von Oberman left. Rogerson returned and poured himself a sherry. He sat down again, sniffed the glass and sipped from it delicately. Drinking in the middle of the day was starting to become a habit. He looked at his watch. He had several more patients to see, a woman in the throes of a nasty divorce and a fifty-year-old banker who hated his life, then a dinner engagement with Philip Marbury at White's that evening.

"Two princes," he mused to himself. "One to help, the other to kill."

Chapter Six

Few, if any members of White's, the oldest and most exclusive club in London, would acknowledge that an Italian of rather low birth founded it. Francis White, who opened White's Chocolate House in 1693, was actually Francesco Bianco, and what he established was not a men's club but a public coffee house. Such are the myths of High Toryism. Aneurin Bevan, the creator of socialized medicine in Britain, described all Tories and presumably all members of White's, as "lower than vermin." When Bevan joined the club, it is reputed that a member kicked him and was then forced to resign. But as Monty Rogerson entered White's at 37 St. James's Street, the worlds of myth and reality blended into a perfect bastion of masculine privilege, notwithstanding the fact that the club gained its prestige under the proprietorship of White's widow, who was known reverentially, as Madame White.

"Over here, Monty," Philip Marbury called cheerfully, waving his hand. He was seated at a table almost directly beneath one of the two ornate chandeliers that graced the dining room. "Hope you don't mind skipping the bar, but I actually have to work tonight."

Rogerson shrugged. Drinking and work were not incompatible to him, but then again, he did not believe that psychiatry required the mental alertness that arguing cases did. He scrutinized Marbury, envying his self-confidence and vibrant good health.

"Have a drink," Marbury coaxed. "Don't mind me."

"I don't like drinking alone when my dinner companion is affecting abstinence."

"All right, then," Marbury signaled to the waiter. "I'll have a Fino. You?"

"Same. You look ridiculously well."

"Well? I feel well."

A grey-haired waiter who looked as old as the club, arrived with the drinks. Rogerson ordered the lobster and Marbury the lamb.

"Fact is," Marbury went on, "I've had a chat with Harrington. We are both of the opinion that perhaps we have gone too far. Closing on the venture we all discussed is going to be more difficult than we thought."

"In what way? I thought it was a done deal."

Marbury polished off his sherry with a flourish.

"They want twenty million pounds. Even Harrington was outraged. The group would have to put it up in advance, with no rebate or return if things don't work out as planned."

"Then it's off?"

"Sorry to say, yes, at the moment."

Rogerson was relieved. He found it hard to believe that he had let himself be sucked into the plot. He imagined himself being led away by the police and then locked up.

Marbury's eyes narrowed as he spoke. "We came close, bloody close. In the event, let's have a good dinner. We'll rethink everything. Harrington may be old and a bit crotchety, but he's no fool, as Lamont-Hope and Waterloo believe. In the meanwhile, we'll look for other opportunities, other arrangements."

The old waiter approached with their food.

"I believe the gentleman ordered the lobster?"

"That's right," Rogerson said.

He put down the dish and then went back to his tray for the lamb.

"Can I interest you gentlemen in some wine? Lobster and lamb might call for a nice rosé. Might I suggest a Domaine Ott, Chateau de Selle 1999?"

"Oh, what the hell," Marbury laughed. "Why not? One does not take rosé seriously, but then again, what does one take seriously?"

"Very good, sir," the waiter bowed.

"The most extraordinary person came in to see me," Rogerson related.

"Really?"

"Yes. Extraordinary. But, of course, I can't say anything about him."

"Well, I know it's a him."

"That's only partially true," Rogerson rejoined.

"I don't know who gets to see the weirdest people, you or I," Marbury chuckled. "What difference does it make as long as they pay us?"

"That's a bit crass."

The waiter placed the bottle in a bucket filled with ice after pouring two glasses. They attacked their meals with gusto, polishing off the rosé as they went.

"Crass? Crass? They even fix cricket matches now. Did you know that cricketers have the highest suicide rate in Britain? It's all part of what I call the Charles syndrome. No standards, the hell with tradition. I suppose we're just stuck with it. We're all just Americans now. There's no use pretending."

The tables in the elegant dining room were all occupied. There was a buzz of male voices in full Anglo-Saxon register, as though India were still the jewel in the crown.

"It's pointless to live in the past," Marbury asserted, draining his glass.

"Are you going wet?" Rogerson questioned.

"Not in the least."

Marbury looked Rogerson in the eye and recited Wordsworth: "For why? Because the good old rule sufficeth them, the simple plan. / That those should take who have the power, / and those should keep who can."

"That's probably still the case," Rogerson acknowledged.

"Not only is it still the case, my dear Monty, it will always be the case. Most people go through life not caring about wealth and power. Those of us who do are special. We're the ones who make things tick, who keep things going. Everyone else is just afraid of dying. But not us. What we fear is dying without what is rightfully ours. Keep that secure and there's nothing to fear. As it stands, this is not the case. A country gone mad with egalitarianism is threatening everything we have. But enough of that for now. As long as we remain vigilant, we will win in the end."

"That's very reassuring," Rogerson sighed.

"Cheer up. The Charles thing is bound to come up again. I'll keep you posted. In the meanwhile, my advice is to relax."

Marbury slapped him on the back as they were leaving the club. It was raining a soft, dismal rain, the kind that engenders the unique brand of English depression experienced by generations of people for whom the stiff upper lip was a way of carrying on when everything seemed meaningless.

"Do you remember the stiff upper lip?" Rogerson remarked. "Whatever happened to it?"

"I'll tell you what happened to it. We stopped being great because some damned fools have convinced everyone that being great is bad. They prefer the tight little island apologizing to the whole world for the empire. Fuck that."

They hailed cabs and went their separate ways, leaving behind the bustling conviviality of White's for the desperate quiet of the London streets.

Chapter Seven

Stanley West puffed on his pipe. His snug little house on Granchester Meadows was filled with memorabilia from his days in the military, including a framed photograph of himself in his major's uniform that he kept on a table in the living room.

West liked institutions that demanded discipline, like the army and the police. He had wanted to be in the air force, but his eyesight was not good enough. He was an orderly, disciplined man who led an orderly and disciplined life. He was rarely without a clean white shirt and tie, even when gardening.

At fifty-eight, he was close to retirement, which he could do comfortably on his two pensions. He loved his little immaculate garden, his basset hounds, and his wife, Margaret, a jolly, lower-middle-class English lady with a pleasant disposition, a double chin and endless energy. They had no children, so lavished their affection on their pets.

Most of all, West liked being English. And like Wellington, he disliked change but recognized that change happened, so there was nothing to do but adjust to it. In this respect, he was not a reactionary, but a conservative. An exception to this was the Euro, to which he swore he could never adjust. His wonderful, old-fashioned unflappable English disposition made him something of an anachronism on the force and he bore the brunt of jokes by his younger colleagues with good humor.

West liked paperwork. Reading reports, such as the one he was currently examining, gave him the opportunity to test his intelligence, on which he prided himself. He never went to university, believing it to be a waste of time, and regarded the new breed of well-educated detectives as suspect. "Over-educated fools" was how he described them. His spectacles down on the tip of his nose, he sat back in his favorite easy chair and studied Michael Rogerson's report like a scientist examining minuscule organisms under a microscope. He had forwarded a copy to New Scotland Yard, but felt himself up to the task of what on the surface seemed a routine matter. Besides, he regarded the Metropolitan Police as overrated, and its reputation unjustified. Indeed, they had left the scene without bothering to arrange for a report on the horse themselves.

According to Rogerson, the Prince of Wales's horse suffered from fractures of the second and fourth metacarpals, "commonly referred to as 'splints.'" The condition had gone unnoticed, he argued, because there was not a "true splint," in which the ligament joining the splint bone to the third metacarpal is torn. Had this been the case, the injury would have manifested itself more readily, allowing for surgical repair, with healing possible after stall rest and physical therapy. "The proper procedure would have been to bandage the leg postsurgically. The horse rested until the sutures were removed and then walked for an additional two weeks, with the leg remaining bandaged for three weeks after the sutures were removed." The object of the physical therapy, Rogerson pointed out, is to reduce inflammation, using systemic and topical anti-inflammatories with warm moist heat alternated with ice-cold therapy and "injections of coricosteroids if necessary."

But this was not possible because the injury went undetected as the result of its being a "blind splint," in which the ligament was inflamed rather than torn, making it more difficult to diagnose. The injury was undoubtedly exacerbated by rapid, hard training on a hard surface, which didn't allow time for the bones, muscles, ligaments and tendons to adjust to the additional stress. There was evidence as well that the leg was bandaged too tightly and not properly shoed. Since the second and fourth metacarpals ("splint bones") are small bones "on either side of the shin," lacking the strength of the third metacarpal or "shin," there "is every reason to conclude that the total fractures happened suddenly, resulting in instantaneous lameness and the fall that injured the Prince of Wales. Since a horse carries most of its weight on its forelimbs, this is where most horse injuries occur, as was the case here, with the front left leg in question."

"The only legitimate course of action at this point was to put the creature out of its misery, which I did with a single gun shot to the head. I disposed of the carcass by sending it to a butcher in Reims for sale as meat, seeing no point in allowing it to go to waste."

Stanley West reread the report several times. He put it down on the table next to his chair and rubbed his chin with his right hand, his left hand cupping the pipe.

"That's all neat and clean," he mused, "very neat and clean, indeed."

"Did you say something, dear?" his wife's high-pitched voice came from the kitchen.

"Just muttering to myself."

West got up and opened the front door. The sun was out.

"I think I'll just go for a stroll," he said.

"Very nice day for that," she responded.

"Indeed."

"Take the dogs."

The two bassets waddled over to him.

"Very well, Sherlock and Moonstone," he coaxed as he put leashes on them.

The three ambled off down the street.

Chapter Eight

Some days later, Monty Rogerson met his brother, Michael, for a rather liquid lunch at the Beefsteak, Michael's club in London.

"Quite a contretemps between the Duke of Edinburgh and the Prince of Wales," Michael chuckled as he polished off yet another glass of Sancerre with his Dover sole.

"Lucky thing for the Prince that he's still alive," Monty offered.

Monty munched on his veal chop. "The way I see it, the Duke has got it exactly right."

"Charles," Michael ordered the waiter, "another bottle."

"Right away, sir," he obeyed sycophantically.

"Are you absolutely certain a white is all right? We could get you a red. What do you say to a nice Pinot Noir, all for yourself?"

Without waiting for a reply, Michael signaled to another waiter.

"Charles, bring us a good Pinot Noir."

"Very good, sir," he responded.

"The Duke," Monty went on, pulling out a newspaper clipping from the *Daily Telegraph*, "is right on the money. Graham Turner says he thinks Charles is 'precious, extravagant, and lacking in the dedication and discipline he will need if he is to make a good king.'"

Michael laughed as both waiters brought the wine. A third waiter came over to inquire if everything was satisfactory.

"Excellent, Charles," Michael nodded.

"At White's, we call the waiters by their given names," Monty challenged.

"How bloody democratic of you. What's the difference? They come, they go, they die. I can't see slobbering all over the place over waiters. A waiter is a waiter. Here, they are all Charles. They don't mind. They actually appreciate the little impersonal touch. They don't have to harbor any illusions that we are in any way sentimental about them. But yes, Prince Philip is right. That Charles is a total fool."

"You're Harrington's vet. What about the horse?"

"You mean the polo pony? A freak accident. I can assure you my report establishes that. It's air-tight. So we're all still stuck with Charles, including his parents. But we've had worse. Just go through the history of the British monarchy. How many great kings have there been? Mostly, they've been a pack of jerks. William IV, now there was a useless twit for you. George IV was a complete nonentity. One could go on. It's the idea of the monarchy that matters, not who's actually king or queen. If you think about it for a minute, we could all have ended up a bunch of Catholic spics if Philip had succeeded. He was married to Mary, after all. Elizabeth was a complete imposter. Without Sir Francis Drake, she would have ended up in a pub, pulling pints. If she were lucky."

"I suppose you're right. Why should I be so obsessed with Charles? It's just that I can't stand the drift, the mediocrity."

"Oh, Monty, don't wallow in that. Just go on doing what you're doing and things will take their course. Blair's not so bad, either. He's defused all the opposition with his phony democratic façade. Scratch the surface and he's one of us."

By the end of lunch, they were both drunk, while pretending not to be. Michael signed for the bill.

"I expect you've got to see some bizarre character who dresses up like a woman while making love to his wife." He quoted: "A homosexual met a lesbian named Sue, / But they did not know just what to do. / On the bed or the floor, or perhaps by the door, / But with what and with which and to who?"

Monty shook his head and smiled.

"Thank you, Charles," Michael said to one of the waiters, who bowed slightly.

"Good day, sir."

Monty Rogerson made his way back to his digs on Eaton Place to find a stunning, distraught blonde woman in stylish clothes waiting for him outside.

"Do we have an appointment?"

"No. But I must see you. I am ready to kill myself."

It was Christian von Oberman.

"I have an appointment in an hour. Come inside."

As they climbed the few stairs to the door, von Oberman exclaimed: "You're drunk."

"If you're going to kill yourself, what difference does that make?"

"I didn't say I was going to kill myself. I said I was ready to kill myself. How can you help me if you're drunk?"

"Stop being so hypercritical. I'm as good at this drunk as everyone else sober. I'm not performing brain surgery."

They entered Rogerson's studio and sat on the sofas. Von Oberman crossed his slim, attractively muscled legs seductively, his skirt sliding up to his thighs. He threw his hair back in a decidedly feminine gesture and lit up a cigarette. In his inebriated state, Rogerson saw a perfectly beautiful and sexually appealing woman gazing at him, the green eyes momentarily mesmerizing him. Von Oberman leaned over and put his hand on his shoulder. Rogerson trembled.

"You're risking quite a lot by walking around like that," Rogerson managed.

"It is now impossible for me to be any other way."

"But we agreed on therapy. You have got to give it a chance."

Von Oberman pulled back his hand: *"C'est bien plus fort que moi."*

"You're German. Whatever happened to the triumph of the will?"

"The same thing that happened to the English stiff upper lip."

Rogerson laughed. "Funny, I just asked someone about that. Why don't we have a little conspiracy? You will get back your will and I will resurrect the stiff upper lip. You can have a perfectly normal life as a man, I can assure you of that. This obsession with becoming a woman has to do with the feminization of the culture. Under this façade you are, in all probability, perfectly masculine. What we've got to work on is what I perceive to be your masochism. I don't mean to be rude, but I do have another patient coming."

"Dr. Rogerson, I have no will to live."

"I can arrange for you to go to hospital, if it's that bad."

"No, no. I couldn't do that. I will be back for our regular appointment."

Rogerson heaved a sigh of relief.

"I would advise a change of clothes. And get rid of the makeup."

Von Oberman looked down sheepishly.

"You think I'm ridiculous."

"Not at all. You've come to exactly the right person. Try to remember your dreams. Get a little book and jot them down. In the meanwhile, try imagining yourself having sex as a man and enjoying it."

"When I'm having sex, I can't decide if I'm a man or a woman."

"We'll discuss that."

Von Oberman got up.

"Do you like St. John Earp?" he changed the subject suddenly.

"Why, yes, I do. Why?"

"I am concentrating on his work. There is an excellent collection at the Fitzwilliam."

"I know. Good. Focus on that. Well, thanks for stopping by."

Von Oberman looked at him.

"You are a very kind man."

"I try."

"But it's not always easy?"

Rogerson didn't answer. He showed von Oberman to the

door.

"Life is not so bad," Rogerson advised.

"Dr. Rogerson, that depends."

After von Oberman's departure, Rogerson, while waiting for his next patient, perused a paper given in 1932 by the psychoanalyst Karen Horney entitled "The Dread of Women." A boy's fear of the father, Horney argued, was a smokescreen for "the fear of the vagina," which was the symbol of motherhood, life, and death. The fear of the vagina had two bases: It is the mysterious place from which life and death originate as well as the sexual goal he will want to pursue. But the boy believes his penis is inadequate to the task, and consequently his sexuality, from the very beginning, is clouded with the terror of rejection, derision and shame. Horney referred to the work of R. Boehm, who, in 1930, defined the "femininity complex" in men as based on "parturition envy," which he described as the envy of the ability to bear and nourish babies and to create life. The complete reverse of Freud's penis envy in women, this involved both "womb envy" and "breast envy."

Rogerson then found a passage in *Sadomasochism* by Susanne Schad-Somers: "In countless folklores and poems, the woman appears as the mysterious other who is both intensely desired, and at the same time, dreaded as the devourer and destroyer."

The struggle to be a man was constant and ongoing, Rogerson believed. In transsexuals, the battle is being lost as the man allows himself to drown his masculinity in a feminine identity. It was, in short, a form of surrender, which, he postulated, was a metaphor for the surrender of British masculinity to the effete. Politically correct British feminism was destroying the country, man by man, until nothing would be left but soft, semi-women like Tony Blair. Rogerson was resolved to save not only von Oberman from his own surrender but all of England from the rapacious claws of the harridans who were transforming the "land of hope and glory" into a quagmire of despair and ridicule. He was having a "Charles attack," as he referred to it.

But beneath this was something Rogerson was not prepared to accept, although it was beginning to caress his conscious state from the depths of his subconscious. He was beginning to fall in love with Christian von Oberman. As he wrestled with this disturbing possibility, he heard the bell ring. It was his next patient, a prominent entrepreneur who had cornered the pizza market in Britain. A tough-looking character with short-cropped black hair, he was convinced that women found him unattractive because he was "too masculine." All his relationships ended disastrously, as one woman after another criticized what they called his "John Wayne" complex. He related to Rogerson how he had broken down in tears after his latest girlfriend walked out on him, advising him to "be more like Tony Blair."

"I hate that bloody fucker!" he shouted at Rogerson.

"Have you thought of dating women from other cultures?"

"Like what?"

"Women from Latin America and China admire masculine men."

"You mean I should date spics and chinks? I'm paying you to be told to fuck spics and chinks?"

"You could do worse."

"How? How could I do bloody worse, Dr. Rogerson?"

"You could keep letting yourself be abused. You don't want that, do you?"

"See you next week, Doc."

He stormed out, leaving Rogerson alone.

Rogerson pondered St. John Earp, an artist whose work he never fully comprehended. He recalled the great, rotund face with the beard and the bald dome as much as the strange art. Known as "Jim," the artist was a surrealist who shocked England in the sixties with his depiction of a dying Christ on a CND (Campaign for Nuclear Disarmament) cross presiding over a last supper on a disintegrating floor. An odd subject for von Oberman, he speculated. Yet Earp was becoming a cult figure whose work had gained an increasing following since his death in 1990 in Brighton.

"Why Earp?" he muttered to himself. "Hmmm. That sounds like Wyatt Earp," he chuckled. Perhaps it was Earp's fascination with the subconscious, his attraction to Freud that made his work compelling to von Oberman as he explored the depths of his own soul. Perhaps von Oberman had also experimented in drugs as a way to reach his inner depths. Freud prescribed opium to his patients, Rogerson was aware. He must remember to ask von Oberman about that.

As he jotted down some notes to himself on his laptop, Rogerson remembered his first encounter with Thomas De Quincy, whose *Confessions of An English Opium-Eater* had greatly impressed him. "Of this, at least, I feel assured that there is no such thing as *forgetting* possible to the mind," De Quincy had written. "A thousand accidents may, and will, interpose a veil between our present consciousness and the secret inscriptions on the mind; accidents of the same sort will rend away this veil, but alike, whether veiled or unveiled, the inscription remains forever; just as the stars seem to withdraw before the common light which is drawn over them as a veil—and that they are waiting to be revealed, when the daylight shall have withdrawn." This was written in 1821. And to De Quincy, it was dreams that revealed the secret inscriptions and opium that lifted the veil.

It was Rogerson's secret that he took opium obtained for him by his brother, which he mixed with water to make laudanum, the Victorian elixir. But he had never induced a patient to try it. Although he did practice psychopharmacology and had several patients on Prozac, it disturbed him that these medications avoided the real issue of getting to the root causes of people's problems. Such medication was the anodyne of psychotherapy, not the archaeology, in his estimation.

The phone rang. It was Philip Marbury.

"Monty, how are the nutcases?"

"Perfectly fine."

"Excellent. We need to meet. There's a new approach. Can you make it later this afternoon? Let's have a stroll through the Tate Modern, say four o'clock."

"I will be there."

"Good. You should like this."

Marbury hung up perfunctorily, leaving Rogerson bemused.

"New approach. I should think so," he muttered.

Rogerson found Marbury standing next to Damien Hirst's split dead cow. He was immaculate in a dark blue, pinstriped, double-breasted suit with double vents and a pair of black shoes so polished, their sheen sparkled like precious gems. His greying hair was smartly brushed back, making his large, pale white forehead even more prominent.

"Take a look at this, Monty," he grinned. "This is what British civilization has come to."

"Did I come here for an art lecture?"

"Don't worry. But this stuff makes Francis Bacon and Lucien Freud look like Renoir. Why is English art so depressing? Do English artists so hate beauty that they think their mission is to destroy it? With Hirst, it's dead split cows, with Bacon, dirty old men in their underwear engaged in sexual combat, and with Freud, it's fat, disgusting women you would not want to get near to under the worst of circumstances. Never mind. Let's take a stroll and I'll fill you in."

They eased past the split cow and a collection of David Hockneys, including a portrait of Henry Geldzahler in his prime.

"Didn't these use to be in the old Tate?" Marbury mused.

They were suddenly confronted with a gigantic painting of Prince Charles as Humpty Dumpty by an artist named Felicite Appleton-Hobart. Charles's crown was being swept away by a huge vulture as a vivid banner proclaimed, "Long Live the Republic!" A grey-haired, matronly woman of about sixty in a tweed suit and brown walking shoes pushed herself in front of the crowd that was examining it, opened her handbag and produced a large kitchen knife, with which she proceeded to slash the painting.

"That bitch is destroying my fucking art!" a small, dark woman in jeans, boots, and a leather jacket screamed.

Several museum guards rushed towards the woman with the knife and swept her away as she shouted obscenities, disarming her and shoving her forward.

"One of us," Marbury quipped. "But she is misguided. In a sense, the artist is right. It is Charles who is producing the republican sentiment."

Marbury winked at Rogerson conspiratorially and guided him by the elbow until they were sufficiently far away from the fracas to address him in a whisper.

"It's the Act of Settlement. It has to be scrapped before the republicans do it."

Marbury expounded on the Act of Settlement of 1701, as they ambled along the corridors. "To be the king, or queen," he asseverated, quoting from text, "you must have the right credentials. It is imperative that you be a descendant of the Princess Sophia, Electress and Duchess dowager of Hanover, daughter of the late Queen of Bohemia, daughter of King James I, to inherit after the King and the Princess Anne, in default of issue of the said princess and his Majesty, respectively; and the heirs of her body, being Protestants…"

"I never knew what that actually meant," Rogerson admitted.

"Primogeniture," Marbury went on. "Sons come before daughters, and sons and daughters of sons come before the offspring of daughters and over the daughters themselves. That's why Prince William is second in line to the throne and Anne is eighth. You must be Protestant, Church of England, descended in the male line, and German. That, of course, violates the Human Rights Act, which we had to adopt because of the European Convention on Human Rights.

"The Council of Europe court can enforce it. The Act of Settlement violates the ban on racial, sexual and religious discrimination. They will bloody force us to have a black lesbian

queen, if they let us have a monarch at all. The republicans
want it all repealed so they can abolish the monarchy straight
out. It's all over the *Guardian*. And Blair has the votes to do
it. His cabinet is made up of a bunch of closet republicans.
They will get rid of the crown and replace it with the Euro.
Our plan is to get the Tories to offer amendments first, retir-
ing the Queen for tolerating Charles's adultery, and making
Charles ineligible to succeed her for violations of the principles of the Church of England.

"The amendments will excommunicate Charles for his unre-
pentant act of adultery. William will be named king. Public
support will be enormous. Blair won't dare to oppose it. We
will organize a giant demonstration in front of Parliament.
There will be total euphoria at the coronation of William. As
soon as he is on the throne, we will get a vote of no confidence in Blair for being a republican. Blair will lose. Then
William will summon the Tory PM and ask him to form a government of national unity."

"A bloodless coup?" Rogerson pondered.

"Exactly. If that doesn't work, well, we can do the other
thing later."

"And the Human Rights Act?"

"Fuck that. The day Europe can tell us who the English
head of state can be is the day it dies. We keep the king, we
keep the pound, and we keep the Church of England. Tory
England will be back."

Rogerson looked up. To his astonishment, they were entering an exhibit of paintings by St. John Earp.

"You know this artist?" Marbury asked.

"Yes. Quite bizarre, actually."

They found themselves gazing at a painting entitled "The
Musician," an ominous, surrealistic portrait of a monstrous,
not-quite-human, hideous troll with a tiny face and simian-like
hands, wearing a strange gold-domed hat like a flying saucer
with a pointed top, and blowing on an ancient macabre pipe-
like instrument with three separate orifices. The backdrop of

a grey and blue misty sky and what appeared to be a crumbling edifice on a barren terrain created a deeply troubling impression of mysterious terror and impending horror, as a strange foreboding object lurked in the foreground.

"What in blazes is that?" Marbury choked.

"A dream?" Rogerson suggested. "We all have our dreams and they are not all pleasant."

"But must we share them?"

"We suppress them at our peril," Rogerson countered.

"Very well," Marbury nodded. "Let's act on ours."

"Acting on your dreams, Dr. Rogerson?" a voice intruded.

Rogerson turned to see a handsome couple, immaculately dressed. It was Christian von Oberman and a stunning brunette of the same height.

"Dr. Rogerson, this is my fiancée, Lady Sarah Filburn. Sarah, this is Dr. Montague Rogerson, the distinguished psychiatrist and aficionado of the work of Jim Earp."

Rogerson duly introduced Philip Marbury. She smiled graciously and shook hands with both men.

"A remarkable show," von Oberman observed. "But please excuse my intrusion. Before we go, Dr. Rogerson, I think perhaps you should join the St. John Earp Society."

"I'll give it some thought."

"We will speak again about it?"

Marbury looked astonished.

"There is a society devoted to this man?"

"Of course," Lady Sarah interjected. "People are only just beginning to appreciate his work. Christian is doing his utmost to see that it is appreciated as it should be."

Von Oberman bowed formally and led Lady Sarah away.

"Strange chap," Marbury commented.

Rogerson rubbed his chin: "You have no idea."

Chapter Nine

"The question is," Philip Marbury explained to an increasingly impatient Viscount Harrington, "whether by proposing the amendments to the Act of Settlement, one commits treason."

"What do you mean 'treason?'" Harrington huffed.

"This would constitute overthrowing the head of state by legislation."

"Oh, balls. Who could do the arresting? This is supposed to be a democracy. Parliament is supreme."

"What if the bloody Queen went on the telly and announced there is no parliamentary authority to abolish the monarchy?"

They were seated in the drawing room of Harrington's posh Albany flat. Harrington puffed deeply on his Coheba and looked up at the ceiling, sinking back into his armchair.

"Does Rogerson suspect anything?"

"He thinks we've called it off. He has no idea we know anything about von Oberman."

"Good. Good. A babe in the woods, that chap. I suspect he never believed we would actually go through with it. Of course, the political route is favorable, but it will take so much longer. No you're right. By doing both, we increase the odds in our favor. And the price?"

Marbury squirmed slightly and stiffened. "Twenty million pounds."

"A drop in the bucket. I'll arrange for you to make the transfer. It's all got to look like it's on the up and up."

"You and the others will be investing it in the Bahamian Luxury Estate Company. That's a subsidiary of Muller Enterprises, the Dutch company that's the parent. Ostensibly, Muller Enterprises is a diversified multinational company with headquarters in St. Maarten."

"They take care of the rest and we keep our distance? But

can they be trusted?"

"Nobody can be trusted," Marbury smiled. "But it will be perfectly constructed."

"We'll need to mobilize the St. George Association for the political stuff."

"Precisely. It's already been launched. Portillo has announced for the leadership of the Tories. Of course, he knows nothing. But that's the first step. Once the leadership business is settled, we can figure out who should introduce the amendments. Blair thinks he owns the country now, but he won't be ready for this."

"How did that little worm get so much power?" Harrington snarled.

"Just remember, Simon, that power is an illusion. We have to create the right illusion."

"It's what I'm paying you to do."

"And worth every penny."

"If someone paid you more," Harrington hissed, "you'd switch sides. Maybe you have already."

"It's true I get paid. I'm a professional. But I get paid only to do what I believe."

A broad grin crossed Harrington's countenance.

"Marbury, if I thought for a minute that you believed in anything, I would never have hired you."

He handed Marbury a Havana.

"Still buying Communist cigars?"

"Listen, Marbury, I do business with Castro. Fact is, he doesn't believe in anything either. The bloody Americans are totally stupid. They keep fighting him when all they have to do is buy him off."

"It all goes back to Kennedy," Marbury explained. "The same policy is still in place."

"I don't blame Castro for getting rid of the Kennedys at all," Harington said. "If you're going to assassinate somebody, a wet affair, you know, you had better bloody succeed. Otherwise, all bets are off."

"Don't worry," Marbury reassured him, as he clipped off the tip of the cigar and lit it up. "The tables won't be turned on you."

"It will be your head if they do," Harrington snapped. "I've seen to that."

"You do see to everything."

"Exactly."

"Did you see that the Andy Warhol portrait of Prince Charles in the Frederick Hughes estate is likely to go for between seventy and ninety thousand pounds at Sotheby's?"

"Pure hagiography," Harrington answered, "if you can say that about a painting. But I think I'll put in a bid."

"Why on earth would you do something like that?"

Harrington smirked. "I need a new dartboard."

At about this time, Stanley West was strolling in the West End, on his way to pay Dr. Michael Rogerson a visit. The train to London had been awful, slow and dirty. A conservative, West did not see privatization of the rail system as progress. Train travel, to West, was inherently English, something that was an organic part of national identity. In his mind, Thatcher and Blair were from the same cut. They did everything they could to undermine national identity for the sake of the marketplace, so that England would be just a smaller version of America.

Having looked everywhere for a pub where he could get a lunch of a Scotch egg and baked beans, he had finally settled on a trendy bistro, where he tried to order fish and chips but was obliged to eat monkfish wrapped in Polish ham at twenty pounds. When he had asked for a half pint of "best bitters," the waitress had stared at him blankly.

"We've got Merlot and Chardonnay by the glass," she explained.

"Can't have a beer?" he pleaded.

She stared back again. "We have Pilsner Urkell from the Czech Republic, by the bottle."

He ordered one, consumed his lunch in silence, and left

with the distinct feeling that the entire world as he knew it was gone.

He was whistling "Get Me to the Church on Time" and puffing on his pipe, an activity that pegged him for what he was, an anachronism, as he looked up and down for the building that housed Rogerson's London veterinary clinic. The small, discreet silver sign indicated that West had reached his destination. He rang the bell, listened for the buzzer and entered the waiting room.

Once inside, Detective Inspector West found himself surrounded by a sea of dogs. Their English masters lavished attention on them, from exotic breeds to mutts. West was not a stranger in this company. He was, by his own admission, like all English people, a fanatical dog lover. A tough law-enforcement man, he nevertheless found himself thinking that Rogerson might not be such a bad bloke after all if he took care of dogs. A horse doctor for Viscount Harrington was one thing, but a dog doctor was another. Just as West made eye contact with the gigantic Great Dane seated opposite him, who eyed him suspiciously, Rogerson's nurse approached him and asked him to follow her. He thus avoided being seduced by a benign façade.

"The doctor will see you now," she informed him.

West picked up his briefcase and followed her down a hall until they reached Rogerson's office. He heard the cries, barks, and whimpering of dogs coming from various examining rooms. The shrill, hysterical scream of a cat shattered the symmetry.

"Come in, West," he heard Rogerson beckon.

Rogerson rose from behind his desk to greet him. He was wearing a white coat and had silver-rimmed glasses on the tip of his nose.

"Not exactly Dr. Doolittle, I'm afraid," Rogerson quipped.

He gestured to West to sit down. West sat opposite Rogerson's desk, opened his briefcase and took out Rogerson's report and his own notes. Rogerson looked at him quizzically, and then eased himself back into his chair.

"The Prince of Wale's polo pony was, I reckon, a healthy animal until the accident," West asserted.

"That's not unusual," Rogerson responded. "This sort of thing happens all the time. It's terribly sad, but if you're going to work a horse that hard, it should come as no surprise."

"But that's precisely the point," West continued. "It would appear that this particular polo pony was not worked hard at all."

"What do you mean?"

"The Prince only recently acquired it. The previous owner, Manuel Bugatz, an Argentinean chap, insists that the horse was fresh. It hadn't run on a hard turf and was quite young. Can you explain that?"

"Detective Inspector West, you seem a bit suspicious," Rogerson commented uneasily. "Besides, I know Bugatz. He's a slimy liar."

"Suspicious? That's part of my line of work, Dr. Rogerson. It's nothing personal, be assured of that. I would be remiss if I didn't follow this up. Apart from the rumors of your drug-dealing, you have a perfectly wonderful reputation. But I needed to put my mind at rest that this was a perfectly ordinary accident, even if it did involve the next in line to the throne."

"How dare you accuse me of drug-dealing," Rogerson coughed, visibly reddening. "Why isn't New Scotland Yard involved if you have such serious misgivings?"

"I didn't say my misgivings were serious. And I didn't accuse you. I said there were rumors to that effect."

"I am a reputable vet. Let me say, West, that I deeply resent this visit."

West fumbled with his pipe.

"I simply thought you might have administered drugs to the horse to increase its performance and that this might have contributed to the event. It is somewhat unusual to get rid of a horse like that. You know what I mean. You sent it to France to be eaten as horsemeat."

"There is a fear of beef these days, West." Rogerson relaxed a bit, "Why waste good horsemeat?" No one eats it in England, which, as far as I'm concerned, is foolishness. So why not send it off to the Frogs?"

"Nothing to cover up, then?"

"Cover up? What would I be trying to cover up?"

West put the documents back in his briefcase and stood.

"I have no idea, really."

Well, I would advise you to call off your fishing expedition," Rogerson barked. "If not, you will hear from my solicitor."

"The thought fills me with terror, Dr. Rogerson," West retorted.

"Look, I'm a very busy man," Rogerson shot back. "I have animals to take care of."

You are aware, are you not, Dr. Rogerson, that they eat dogs in Vietnam and China? If one of your patients were run over by a car, would you send it off to be made into canine Schezuan?"

Rogerson bit his lower lip. "I won't bother to respond to that."

"No need," West replied as he stood up to go. "I certainly regret having caused you any inconvenience."

West departed without shaking hands, walking through the waiting room to the cacophony of barking dogs. Rogerson immediately got on the phone.

"That absurd, meddling detective, Stanley West has just gone. He suspects something," he wheezed into the phone.

"Stay calm," Lamont-Hope advised. "He knows nothing and he can prove nothing."

"I'm not so sure."

"Sit tight," Lamont-Hope ordered. "Harrington can fix anything, if it comes to that."

"I'm not so sure," Rogerson said, hanging up.

West took the tube, which was dirty and foul-smelling, to New Scotland Yard at Broadway, S.W.l. for his meeting with Detective Superintendent Sheila Robinson, a red-haired, slim woman with a milk-white complexion and grey eyes. West pulled out his copy of Rogerson's report and proceeded to describe the information he had obtained from Manuel Bugatz.

"We are, I'm afraid, Detective Inspector West, a bit dubious about Bugatz. He has a record of selling damaged polo ponies. He was virtually run out of America. The complaints against him are a mile long. Besides, Forensics has examined the report and found nothing suspicious. Neither has Special Branch."

West had the distinct impression that she was being condescending. He was not particularly glamorous, it was true, but he was competent. Years of police work had led him to have confidence in his hunches, even if at first blush, there seemed to be no bases in fact for them. This was the exact opposite of what good police work was, which he knew meant the application of commonsense to facts. But what if the facts were themselves misleading, or if they hinted at things he could not substantiate? West was like a good police dog that picked up a scent and then followed it to where it led.

"We are talking here about the Prince of Wales," he declared solemnly. "He might have been killed. My guess is that Rogerson administered drugs to the horse to enhance its performance."

"There is no evidence of that, Detective Inspector West. I have checked with the Drug-Related Violence Intelligence Unit, and they can find nothing on Rogerson. And the horse has been disposed of."

She smiled at him like a schoolteacher at a child who has given a wrong answer but stubbornly clings to it.

"That's precisely the point," West said.

"Detective Inspector West, we appreciate your concerns. This did involve the Prince of Wales, but he is doing well. In fact, he wishes that this entire matter be dropped. He doesn't like the publicity, which undermines his reputation as a horseman. The Queen also finds the matter to be distasteful. The Royal Family does not wish to appear to be paranoid."

West was becoming increasingly uncomfortable. He thought it best not to bring up the unsubstantiated rumors that Rogerson provided drugs to well-heeled clients, who paid his exorbitant fees to look after their pets. In an attempt to appear confident, he pretended to fiddle with his pipe, which was unlit. The ploy failed. He realized that his gesture only made Detective Superintendent Robinson appear even more benevolently patronizing.

"Look, West, I don't mean to undermine your work," she purred, as she leaned over her desk towards him, "but as far as we're concerned this was an accident. Polo is a dangerous sport and we wish Prince Charles would give it up. But that's not our business. If he wants to go and break his neck, there's not much we can do about it. Why don't you simply enjoy the rest of the day in London? Do you get to town often? I expect not. Catch a show, have yourself a nice meal somewhere. I certainly appreciate your stopping in."

Her accent was clipped and sharp, but definitely not upperclass. She might have been Anne Robinson dressing down a fumbling contestant on "The Weakest Link." Robinson got up and walked around her desk, gently putting her hand on his shoulder.

"You must be close to retirement," she offered.

West became visibly agitated. "I'm not bloody senile," he half-shouted.

"Oh, dear, West, I'm not suggesting that. But police work has changed. We rely less on intuition and more on science."

"Einstein," West rejoined, "intuited the universe. He had absolutely no basis in fact for relativity."

"He did do the math," Robinson parried.

There was no winning this argument. West held out his hand, which she shook firmly.

It was raining when he walked out onto the street.

"Bloody London," he muttered to himself. "Catch a show, my foot."

When he returned home, Sherlock and Moonstone jumped

up on him, displaying the strange basset characteristic of subdued affection and insistence that you do something for them.
Moonstone ran to a small box and grabbed a tug of war with
his mouth, charging back at West with it.

Mrs. West called from the kitchen: "How did it go at New
Scotland Yard, Stanley?"

West was soaking wet. He stood in the middle of the room,
tugging back as Moonstone growled and Sherlock continued
to jump up on him in his pursuit of a treat.

"It went rather poorly," West sighed. "She thought I was
a fool."

"Well, whatever you may be," she shouted, "you're not a
fool. The Cambridge police know that. They have no right to
treat you like that."

West sank into his chair, disheartened.

"Singh phoned," she continued. "He wanted to remind
you about chess tomorrow night."

Ashook Singh was a dentist with whom he played chess.

It will do you good," she continued. "Singh knows you're
not a fool."

"That's terrific news," West muttered. "Terrific news."

Chapter Ten

The night of West's chess game with Ashook Singh, race riots broke out in a number of cities. Mobs of white supremacist skinheads, under the banner of the British National Party, confronted Asian youths as vandals smashed windows of stores owned by Asians.

"I did not think," Singh pondered, as he gazed at the chessboard contemplating his next move, "that there would a Kristalnacht in England."

"This is a small minority. It is not England," West responded.

"Over eleven percent of the vote in Burney is not a small minority. The Nazis never won a majority in Germany, but they managed to take power all the same. Hague and the Tories must take some of the blame. They whipped up hatred of immigrants. If this is the road to power, England is finished. English civilization is a thin veneer."

Singh moved a bishop across the board, challenging West's king. West took a deep breath.

"What have we here, an attempted assassination? Regicide will not do, Singh."

"Only once in this country was there regicide, my dear West. They lopped off Charles I's head and this country is still reeling."

Singh was a wiry, intense man with a gaunt face but with a seemingly benign nature. Yet he played chess like a killer.

"These mobs," he continued, "are capable of doing anything. The façade of England is crumbling."

West moved a knight in front of his king so that if Singh took it, West would take it with the king.

"That is the secret of England," Singh quipped. "Power is always protected by its flunkies."

Singh moved a rook, so that if West's king took the bishop, the rook would take the king.

"The castle," West smiled, "is, after all, an offensive weapon."

"Those of us from the former colonies have learned the ways of the master. Your days are numbered. Checkmate is not far off."

West moved a pawn forward, throwing Singh's game plan into disarray.

"The entire world underestimates the English," West rejoined. "Right here in this little game, I have outfoxed you."

Several moves later, West had Singh's king cornered.

"Very well, West, I resign. I have been distracted by the violence. To tell you the truth, I feel threatened."

"That is why we have the police," West replied. "There is violence everywhere. England is no exception."

"But what if the police cause the violence?"

"That will never happen in England," West concluded.

They set up the board for another game, which Singh won quickly.

"Ah, I have got it back. You reassure me, West. You are the best kind of Englishman. You don't pretend to be what you are not. Have you straightened out that horse business?"

Singh's wife appeared silently with a tray of sweets. West gobbled up a few and nodded his thanks.

"I've run into a stone wall," he lamented.

"Well, you must bump up against it," Singh's wife commented, "until you have smashed it down."

"That is easier said than done," West observed. "English walls have a way of being particularly impervious."

Singh grinned at West. "That is because the English know best how to conceal power. Power is most effective when it is concealed."

"I don't conceal bloody anything," West snapped.

"So you don't have any power," Singh added, as he put away the chess set. "Only a few have power in England."

"I wonder, Singh, why, if you find this country so distasteful, you choose to live here?"

Singh stared back at him. "I will forget that you ever said that," he responded. "But I will tell you, plain and simple. I live here because it is a better life."

West was flustered. "I'm no bloody racist."

"Well, a bit insensitive, perhaps. Let us leave it at that. But as I said, you don't pretend to be what you are not."

"I am pretending to be what I am not," Christian von Oberman wept, while Montague Rogerson listened. As usual, they sat on the two sofas, with von Oberman periodically reaching for a tissue to wipe his eyes.

Von Oberman related what he referred to as his "feminine discomforts."

"What I feel, Dr. Rogerson," he sobbed, "is that I am pregnant. My prostate gland, though perfectly normal, needs to rid itself of something. I confess that sometimes I smoke hashish and when I do, I sense that my testicles and penis have disappeared inside my body and that I have developed breasts. Today, I wear only the mask of manhood. In all other aspects, and in every part of my body, I feel myself to be a woman."

"Your mother," Rogerson interjected. "Tell me about your mother."

"We have been inseparable since the very beginning. She is a brilliant and very accomplished person. Her doctorate is in philology and she has published several books. Her lectures at Freiburg were famous. Yet she always had time for me, more than enough time. We often slept in the same bed together, even when my father was home. She would spend part of the night with me, and then go back to him.

"My father is a surgeon and was often unable to come home for dinner because of emergencies. Those were special nights because we would be alone together until the morning. Also, my father has many hobbies that kept him from us. Fly-fishing is one of his passions. He needed this because of the stress of his occupation.

"My mother always told me I was more important to her than he was, that notwithstanding his enormously successful career and his station in life, she did not respect him. He had been in the Hitler Youth, for which my mother had contempt. She thought the Nazis were déclassé. Most of all, my mother regretted that she had not been born a man."

"She was both mother and father to you?"

"My mother was, and is, everything to me," von Oberman replied.

"How do you feel about Sarah?"

"Dr. Rogerson, when I am with Sarah, she is the man and I am the woman. She is a very strong woman, very much like my mother. I am in love with her. I think I could be happy with her to a point. We could have children. I love children even more than I love art."

Rogerson took a deep breath. He was feeling the effects of the opium.

"You look tired, Dr. Rogerson. We have only a few more minutes. I would understand if you wanted to stop."

"No, no, I'm fine. Art is very important to you?"

"I regret also that I am not an artist. I have no capacity to create. What I have is the capacity to understand art and to authenticate it. Art is mystery. Authentication is science. Ultimately, there is no explanation for how it is created. Do you know why rich people are prepared to pay so much for art? They are not buying an investment. What they are doing is trying to be near something they cannot be, no matter how much money they have. Wilde was right. Art has no use whatsoever."

"It has a use," Rogerson demurred. "It keeps you sane."

"That is by no means a certainty."

"I think we have done enough for today," Rogerson remarked, getting up unsteadily.

He walked von Oberman to the door. Before he departed, von Oberman turned to him and said, "I'm serious about the

St. John Earp Society. It would mean a lot to me if you joined. Will you?"

"Something to think about," Rogerson answered.

Once out on the street, von Oberman took out a tiny cell phone from his jacket pocket. He waited for a moment before speaking into it:

"This is Ramos. Everything is on schedule."

Chapter Eleven

Singh finished up with his last patient of the day. He was look-ing forward to a quiet evening at home with his wife, which is how he spent most evenings when he wasn't playing chess. His ritual was to walk the one block from his office on Trumpington Street to the bus stop, which deposited him about a quarter of a mile from his house, and then walk home. This was his only exercise, but he deemed it sufficient as long as he "contemplated it with sufficient intensity," as he told others.

He was alone on the street. As he approached the bus stop, he found himself obstructed by five young men, all skinheads with tattoos and earrings.

"What's a bloody nigger doing on Trumpington Street?" the smallest one demanded.

"I can't imagine," said another, mockingly.

A third one shoved Singh: "Bloody nigger. Fucking wog."

"Excuse me," Singh said. "I am going to the bus."

"He's going to the bus," one of them sneered.

"The nigger is going to the bus," the last one snarled.

"Yes, I am going to the bus."

"I don't bloody think so," the first one challenged. He had a club.

"Please, let me go," Singh pleaded. "What have I done to you?"

One of them pushed Singh again. "I'll tell you what you did. You fucking came here, that's what you fucking did, you fucking cunt."

"If you want money, I will give you money."

Singh fumbled for his wallet and took out the bills, hand-ing them over to a skinhead.

"How much has he got?"

"Thirty-six pounds."

"Thirty-six pounds?" they all laughed.

"How much has he got hidden in his pants?" the tallest one asked. "If you show us what you've got in your pants, we'll let you go."

They attacked Singh, clubbing him and beating him with their fists until he lay on the ground defenseless in a fetal position. After kicking him hard with their boots, one of them crushed Singh's skull with his foot. Blood oozed from his nose and ear.

"The nigger's dead," someone growled.

They tore off down the street and around a corner and were gone.

Eventually someone came along, saw the body and phoned the police. Stanley West was assigned to the case and rushed to the scene to see his friend dead and bloody. His first thought was that he would have to notify Singh's wife, Doli. He ordered the site of the crime sealed off and the body taken for an autopsy. It would also be examined for signs of fingerprints. Then a slow rage began to burn in him like a thin, white flame.

He knew an England that was safe, where the criminals didn't commit gratuitous acts of violence, and where, if two murders happened in a year, it was a lot. Long regarded as the apotheosis of English civilization, Cambridge was no longer safe to walk around in at night. Muggings were routine happenings. Violent crimes, many of them drug-related, were increasing at a rapid rate.

If Dr. Michael Rogerson and the thugs who committed this despicable act were not related in fact, they were related, in West's mind, in spirit. The old order, in which certain things were simply not done, had given way to a kind of cynical nihilism that was a bad imitation of America. West's Tory England was a place in which decency and fairness prevailed, whatever differences the classes had amongst themselves. The very existence of class presupposed that everyone belonged somewhere, and it was that sense of belonging that imbued the country with a civility that made it unique in the world.

West had experienced the hurts of the class system but they could be dealt with. It was possible to be upwardly mobile in the English class system, a fact that was never grasped by the Americans. It was not a caste system such as they had in India. In the days of the Teddy Boys, there had been some gratuitous violent crime, but never on this scale. Even the mods and rockers had their limits.

In England, West believed, viciousness was bred out of the people the way it had been bred out of bulldogs. But now a bobby without a gun was a bobby in danger. He recalled his remark to Singh, the one Singh said he would ignore. Yes, it was the presence of the immigrants that was causing this. As long as England remained a white country, there was community on a national scale. People cared for each other, as long as there was no mass culture to sweep away the organic traditions that bound the country together and no all-pervasive technology to make people redundant. What was the word West was looking for? "Dehumanized," he muttered to himself.

His eyes narrowed as he watched them carry away Singh's body. Had he, himself, been poisoned by an inability to extend community to others different from himself? Are those increasing differences the source of the violence that so bothered him, West wondered?

Instead of phoning, he decided to go to Singh's house and tell his wife what had happened.

"Stanley, what are you doing here now? There is no chess. You play again next week. Ashook should be home any moment. If you like, I can get you something to drink."

Neither of the Singhs drank alcohol but they kept some on hand for guests.

"No thank you, Doli," West mumbled, as he rocked awkwardly from foot to foot.

"Something has happened. What has happened?"

"Doli, I'm afraid… I'm afraid that Singh has had a terrible accident."

"He is all right? He has been hit by an auto?"

"Not that, Doli, Singh was mugged. He's dead."

She began pounding on his chest with her fists, crying uncontrollably.

"No, no, this is a lie. You mean they robbed him?"

"Evidently."

"Who did this horrible thing? What will I do? I must see him."

West was confused and disoriented. What, if anything, held England together now? Were there still common symbols with which people could identify? There had been the crown, the pound, the Church of England, the once Holy Trinity of Tory England. Who cared about any of them anymore?

"You will have to identify the body. Once the inquest is over, you can arrange for the funeral."

Doli was numb.

"I can drive you over to identify him," West explained. "Later, I will have to ask you some questions."

"Of course. When this is over, I don't know what I will do. I am not home here and I am not home in India. I have no life anywhere."

"We will find the killers," West tried to reassure her.

When Doli saw Singh's battered body and crushed head, she collapsed. West put his hands over his eyes. He was weeping.

"I have a cousin in America, in New Jersey. I will go and live with her there."

She was barely audible.

"I can drive you home, Doli. You can't stay here."

The silent drive back was like a funeral cortège. Doli did all she could to contain herself. She got out of the car unsteadily and walked to her door.

"Doli, you know where to reach me," West said, as he got ready to drive off.

She disappeared into the house, a solitary figure with drooping shoulders.

As West drove away, he began to think about how, if he could have his way, he would execute the perpetrators. He believed in capital punishment and insisted that only the authorized cruelty of the state could prevent this kind of mayhem. In this regard, he was, again, out of step with his culture. The European Community banned capital punishment, and Britain was part of that community. He felt powerless. Singh had been right. He had no power. Only the few had power. They could do whatever they wanted.

He would have to devote most of his time to this assignment, but he was determined not to let Michael Rogerson off the hook, whatever the bureaucratic fools thought at New Scotland Yard.

His wife and the dogs greeted him when he got home.

"It's terrible," she told him.

"You know about Singh?"

"It was on the news. Stanley, why don't you retire now?"

He became visibly irritated.

"How could I possibly do that? This was Singh."

"I suppose you're right, but it isn't getting any better. You could get killed, that's all I mean. Things aren't what they used to be, that's for sure."

West turned on the television. The reporter was recounting the story of Singh's murder again.

"The City of Cambridge has been rocked by the violent murder of Ashook Singh, a dentist. So far, there are no clues and no suspects. Anyone with any information is advised to report it to the police at once. Meanwhile, rioting continued across the north of England, with gangs of young whites fighting with Asians. And in London, supporters of the monarchy of the St. George Association clashed with an angry mob of anti-monarchists of the Cromwell Brigade in front of Buckingham Palace. Police dispersed the rioters, using teargas. No one was seriously hurt, although several people were taken to hospital. In Belfast, the IRA issued a warning that it will again refuse to disarm, as Ian Paisley, of the pro-unionist party, declared that the time had come to disarm them forcibly. Prime Minister Blair has announced that he will address the nation tonight on television at 9:00 PM to discuss today's events."

Precisely at nine, Tony Blair, looking haggard and nervous, spoke from behind his desk into the television camera. He seemed oddly diminished for someone who had recently won a landslide victory.

"Today's shocking murder of a British subject of Indian descent has outraged all of us. This is intolerable behavior that can and will never be acceptable. Violence can never be condoned. We live in a constitutional system in which human rights are respected and protected. The perpetrators of violent crimes will be hounded down, caught and punished to the fullest extent of the law.

"A small minority is fostering the bigotry and racism that has inflamed the country. These people are mistaken if they think they can destabilize a civilized society. I want to assure the people of this great nation that this government is in control. It has been returned to power by a great majority of the voters and it will remain in power until such time as the electorate wishes otherwise. Whatever changes are going to be made in the United Kingdom will be made through parliament in a democratic fashion. No one, and I mean no one, has the right to decide that he can take the law into his own hands to accomplish his objectives. The entire world is looking at Britain. What do you wish them to see? Do you want them to see the world's leader in human rights and respect for human dignity and law and order, or a chaotic, hostile, and anarchic country that has no basis for criticizing Rwanda?

"The choice is so obvious as to make the very suggestion that there is one ludicrous. I have called on the police to use whatever means are necessary to restore order and to quell violence. Our hearts go out to Mrs. Singh at this terrible moment, whose husband was a distinguished and gentle man."

When Blair finished speaking, Waterloo and Lamont-Hope hurled their glasses at the television screen in Lamont-Hope's rooms.

"Get rid of that ponce!" Lamont-Hope shouted.

"One thing at a time," Waterloo replied.

"I'm tired of waiting," Lamont-Hope complained.

Sir Adrian got himself another glass and filled it with whiskey.

"David, stop being a schoolboy. Things are moving along. Have patience."

Lamont-Hope pursed his lips.

"I want my country back," he said.

"I can assure you that you will have it."

Part Two

Chapter Twelve

"Rude boy" was Jamaican for the Kingston thugs who terrorized the Establishment. Bob Marley, who became a symbol of peace and nonviolence, had started out as a "rude boy." It was through the threat of violence that he got his first recordings played by disk jockeys. The disease of the colonized had come back to haunt the colonizers. Now, the white thugs of the former mother country were the "rude boys." And now, Stanley West was obliged to descend into the underworld of Rude Britannia in pursuit of Singh's killers.

West needed to recruit somebody from the milieu he could trust. But how could he do it? He took to hanging out at tough pubs and engaging people in conversation, but his presence was incongruous. In The Dragon, on Clarendon Street, where ear-splittingly loud Radiohead CD's blasted above the din of the shouting and cursing crowd that packed it, Thom Yorke was howling, "Release me! Release me!" as West found himself seated at the bar next to a tall girl in her late teens. She had straight black hair and wore skin-tight jeans with a tough black belt with a metalic buckle and a black leather motorcycle jacket with a Swastika on the back. Her pale white skin was translucent and her dark eyes were heavily made up with mascara and long, artificial eyelashes. Her eyebrows were perfectly arched. Her white T-shirt fit tightly around her small, firm breasts and was pulled up sufficiently to reveal her belly button, which was pierced with a piece of gold jewelry.

Her high cheekbones gave her face the allure of a fashion model, were it not for the uneven teeth. She wore cut-off gloves that resembled brass knuckles and one long silver earring from her left earlobe. Her body was taut and thin and she was coiled on the bar seat like a venomous snake. West looked down at her feet to see boots of the kick-ass variety.

"What you doin' here, pops?" she intoned in a Cockney accent. She had an aura of insouciant, menacing hostility. Dense cigarette smoke swirled about her as she took a deep drag on a Players. After inhaling deeply, she blew the smoke into West's face. "It's past your bedtime."

West coughed uncomfortably. "I'm looking for Ashook Singh's murderers."

"Don't look at me, mate. I don't bloody know nothing."

"But you've got the Nazi symbol on your jacket. Why would you wear something like that? You are English?"

"English? English? What in bloody hell does that mean? I got nothing against Hitler. Seems to me he got it right. Nobody does fuckin' nothing for you in this country if you're white. You gotta bloody do it for yourself, right? This Ashook Singh, I heard about 'im and I figured, so what? It ain't my bloody business."

She stubbed her cigarette out and West handed her another.

"Well, thanks anyway," she grabbed it. West offered her a light and she leaned over to let the flame do its job.

"Get you another drink?" West offered.

"Yeah, why not? It's rum and coke. Funny, huh? I picked that up when I was in Cuba."

West looked astonished. "You were in Cuba?" He ordered her drink and a pint for himself.

"Yeah. Funny story how I got there, me and a couple of other blokes."

"Were you working?"

"Kinda, you might say that. But it's a bit more complicated."

Radiohead was droning "Pyramid Song" without conviction.

"Do you like this music?"

"Nah. That's the point. Not to like it. Not to like ANYF-ING, really, because it's all shit, in't it? We were hanging out in this bar in London, and some Spanish guy, Cuban actually, comes up to us. There's this gig in Havana. We go to Havana and bring stuff back to the U.K. and drop it off. No drugs or stuff like that. Stupid stuff they want at the embassy. Stuff for cooking that they can't get in London, spices and stuff. They don't like to bring it in themselves because customs always opens it all up and spills it on the floor, even with so-called diplomatic immunity. As foreigners, they're suspect. But as we're English, they figure we can get through with it, and they were right. So over there, I start drinking rum and Coke. They've got plenty of Coke, even with the embargo. It comes in from Mexico. They paid us in pounds. And the truth is, I never liked English beer. Tastes like bloody piss."

West was scrutinizing her, looking for an opening.

"Is there anything you wouldn't do for money?" he asked.

"I wouldn't suck your dick." She spit it out like poison.

West cringed, then composed himself.

"As I said, I'm looking for Ashook Singh's killers. I am prepared to make this worth your while."

"For example."

"A thousand pounds."

West was prepared to use his own money and had no intention of doing this officially. She sat silently, brooding over his proposition. Before she had time to respond, he handed her his card.

"To whom have I had the pleasure of speaking?" he added.

She picked up a napkin from the bar, pulled a pen from her jacket pocket and scribbled, "Molly Stock," adding a phone number and an e-mail address.

"When do I get the fucking cash?"

West produced an envelope and thrust it at her. "You've just got it."

Without saying another word, Molly stuffed the envelope into her jeans and slid from the chair. She waved to someone and walked off, leaving West at the bar.

"Get you another one?" the publican inquired solicitously.

"That will do for tonight," West quipped.

"Thought you was going to pick up that tart, wot?"

"So did I," West lied. "She had other fish to fry."

"She's a mean one," the publican continued. "I've seen her in fights. She's bloody vicious. She punched out a guy right here in the bar the other night. He put his hand on her knee and she let 'im 'ave it. Knee to the groin and it was over, but she finished 'im off with a right upper cut. Consider yourself lucky. She'd 'ave lifted your wallet and then slit your bloody throat."

West had gone on his hunch. She was a killer, but he sensed something else. What was it? Not conscience, that was for sure. Fear? Did she even know the meaning of the word? He had gambled and would have to wait. Singh. He thought about his friend. Was there something he was missing? Then it came to him. Was someone sending him a message? A boy, no more than sixteen, ambled over to him and put his hand on West's shoulder. He was emaciated and had several teeth missing. His head was shaved except for a bit of black stubble on his scalp.

"'Aving a few pints with the hoi polloi, right?"

"Just relaxing," West explained.

The kid stared into West's eyes. "If I was you, I wouldn't be relaxing." Then he darted off.

West left the money for the drinks on the bar. He caught one last glimpse of Molly, who was smoking furiously at a table filled with grinning youths who were drinking heavily. Another girl was laughing, her head thrown back. Her blonde hair was cropped short and she had a gold ring in her nose. "Release me! Release me!" again. They all joined in, off-key, waving their arms in drunken revelry.

When West got home, Margaret and the dogs were already asleep. They did not stir. The dogs knew when he came in at night, recognizing the nuances of his movements. If it had been a stranger, they would have dashed down, barking furiously. A solitary light was on as he maneuvered his way toward the telephone table on which the answering machine sat, the red light flickering on and off. He pressed the button and waited.

"This is Molly Stock. I have some information for you. Meet me tomorrow afternoon, one o'clock, in front of the Varsity. When you see me, just keep walking."

That was it. He went upstairs and into the bathroom, feeling queasy from the cigarette smoke. Pipes and cigars were pleasant to him, but cigarettes turned his stomach. He smelled of them from The Dragon. He took off his suit jacket and brushed his teeth. Then he crept into the bedroom and finished undressing, hanging his suit in the closet. Margaret always put his pajamas on top of the pillow on his side of the bed. He found them, got into the bottom and then buttoned up the top.

If Stanley and Margaret had sex ten times a year, it was a lot. At that, it was always perfunctory, with Margaret bouncing her bottom up and down until he had a very minor orgasm. "Thank you, Stanley," she always said afterwards, as if he had just given her a ham sandwich. It was not anything he particularly relished, but he loved Margaret for being so appreciative of him. She was simply not an erotic being and never had been. Sex was something that barely figured in their kind of English relationship, which endured out of inertia and mutual regard.

What West enjoyed when he got into bed was the sound his bassets made as they slept. It was a low hum, a kind of benign snoring that calmed and lulled him to sleep. But that night he was particularly agitated. The entire episode at The Dragon confounded him. He knew this world existed. It was part of his work to know that it did. But every time he confronted it, he felt he was experiencing one more nail in the coffin of England. The way Molly Stock put down England sickened him. To him, England was the country that twice saved Europe in the twentieth century.

It reminded him of a film he had seen recently called *Sexy Beast*. Everyone hated England in that film. If he were to judge by that film, the country was rotten with corruption and the people in it were psychotic maniacs. All anyone wanted to do was escape: Spain was paradise, England hell. He had been to Spain once on holiday and the sun had turned his pink flesh beetroot. He had come down with a terrible case of diarrhea and vowed never to return.

Finally he fell asleep fitfully, to be wakened by Margaret, who was shaking him gently. It was morning and she was standing over him in a dressing gown.

"Stanley, dear, you slept ever so badly last night. It's Singh, isn't it?"

"I met this girl last night when I was out looking for clues. She was positively evil."

"Stanley," she went on, "there is evil. It exists. You know that. The ones who killed Singh are evil. But everything isn't evil. But it does smell like you've been to hell and back. Get up and have some breakfast. You'll feel better."

West didn't tell Margaret that he had given Molly a thousand pounds of their money. The thought that it might have been for naught troubled him. He would find out at one o'clock. He dressed and went downstairs, where Margaret had started cooking bacon, eggs, and fried bread. They ate silently, West smothering his toast with Robertson's orange marmalade. Sherlock and Moonstone ran around the table, looking for crumbs.

The phone rang. It was Molly.

"Just checking. You got my message?"

"Yes."

"You've got to give me more," she demanded.

"More what?"

"More money."

"I can't do that."

Margaret pretended not to be listening. She picked up the newspaper and buried her head in it.

"When you get to the Varsity, have it ready in another envelope so I can see it. If I can't, I will disappear."

She hung up abruptly.

Margaret reappeared from behind the newspaper.

"Who was that, dear?"

"That terrible girl I met last night. She says she has some information."

"Well, you never know," Margaret sighed. "You're meeting her today?"

"Yes. One o'clock."

"Well, be careful, Stanley. She's probably going to lie."

West looked puzzled. "Why would she do that?"

"It was you who said she was evil," Margaret reminded him. "Of course she'll lie."

Somehow, West thought not. He took out his pipe, filled it with tobacco, and lit it.

"We shall see," he nodded.

West had a sandwich for lunch at his desk. Then he went over to the Varsity, a restaurant in the middle of Cambridge that had been there for decades. He walked slowly, holding the envelope absentmindedly in his left hand. Molly was in her same outfit. She looked as if she had probably slept in it. She began walking and he began following her, finally striding alongside her as they talked.

"How much?" she solicited.

"A hundred pounds."

"A hundred quid? Why don't you make it in fucking Euros."

"Listen," he snapped, "have you got anything or not? Eleven hundred pounds is not peanuts."

West was rapidly growing impatient. Margaret was probably right.

She stopped in her tracks, grabbed the envelope from him, and turned right at him, her face practically touching his.

"First, I never said NUFFING to you, and I never got NUFFING from you. Second, I never told you NUFFING. But this is it. They didn't do it alone. Someone put them up to it. Now fuck off."

She turned and ran.

"Wait!" West cried out, but it was no use. She was gone.

West kept walking, absorbing what she had told him. He pulled out his cell phone, which he despised, and punched in Molly's number. He got her voicemail.

"This is Stanley West. I have to speak with you. I could call you in, but I would rather not. It would be best if you e-mailed me. It would be unwise to withhold information."

He left his e-mail address on the message machine and put the phone back in his jacket. He sensed she wasn't lying, that there was more to it than a gratuitous act of violence by a gang of thugs. He walked aimlessly until he found himself on King's Parade, in front of King's College, staring up at the chapel. D. H. Lawrence had described it as a "dead sow on its back," but West found it majestic, even inspirational. He went inside to the dark silence and saw a solitary figure in a pew. He recognized instantly that it was Molly. West approached her cautiously.

"Molly?"

"Who fucking else?" she snapped.

"Have you been praying?" West inquired.

"You've got to be joking. Just catching me breath. I got NUFFING more to say to you. You want to find out more, hang out at The Dragon. But I'd watch my back if I was you."

An Anglican priest hushed them. He was tall, gaunt, and bent, with a mane of white hair.

"If you must talk, please go outside," he admonished. He bowed deeply before the cross and exited hastily through a side door.

West followed Molly outside until they were in front of the Gibbs building. He sensed that she was in crisis.

"I can't tell you any more. I can't. I can't."

"You do know more?"

"I said that was it. I don't know nuffing more."

"You're lying," West blurted out, remembering Margaret.

"Look, they'd bloody kill me if they knew I was talking to you. I told you what you wanted to know and you bloody paid me. Now leave me alone."

"You're an informer now," West admonished. "You might as well accept that. The only security you can have is by telling me everything. Once we've got Singh's killers, you will be out of danger."

"Bloody hell I will be," she shot back.

It was drugs, for sure, West concluded. Molly Stock needed the money for drugs. She would need more.

"What are you on, Molly, horse?"

"That's none of your fucking business."

"I can arrange to take care of your habit."

"I'm not going to no bloody rehab."

"I didn't say that," West cajoled. "I said I would take care of it."

"In exchange for everyfing?"

"Exactly," West replied.

"I need time to fink."

"We don't have much time," West insisted.

"That's your bloody problem, in't it?"

West knew he couldn't have her arrested. He had compromised himself out of anger. He had to play along, like having a fish precariously on a line. He had played her hard and knew he had to let up slack.

"You can e-mail me, as I said in my phone message. You know the address?"

"I got the bloody message. If I've got more to tell you, I'll let you know. And I'll let you know how much it will cost."

This time, he let her take off without thinking of following her. On his way back to the office, he picked up a newspaper. Back at his desk, he flipped through it. He never knew what he would find in the media. A photograph with a brief news story caught his eye. The headline read: "DISTINGUISHED PSYCHIATRIST NAMED AS HONORARY CHAIRMAN OF THE ST. JOHN EARP SOCIETY."

It was Dr. Montague Rogerson. The article described St. John "Jim" Earp as a visionary and mystic whose work was being actively promoted by the Society and its members, which included German art expert Prince Christian von Oberman. Rogerson was quoted as saying that his interest in the artist stemmed from "Earp's dreamlike landscapes that evoke a symbolism I find closely related to Freud's dream analysis and the early psychological theory of the twenties and thirties." He likened looking at an Earp to "entering on a voyage of discovery in much the same way as psychoanalysis and psychotherapy enable one to do."

West underlined the name "Rogerson," clipped the article, folded it, and put it in his pocket. When he got home, Margaret greeted him with the question he expected.

"She lied, didn't she?"

"Why are you so sure?" he asked back. "Sometimes you just have to trust the most unlikely people. In fact, the more unlikely they are, the more likely it is they're telling the truth."

Margaret was making shepherd's pie, a sort of English moussaka, with soft mashed potatoes spread over ground meat and baked. It had been a staple at English restaurants for years, but was now part of the vanishing act of a bygone era, like saying something "wasn't cricket." It wasn't possible to imagine Robin Cook eating shepherd's pie. Jeffrey Archer used to serve it at his lavish champagne parties, but only as a joke. West was convinced that Margaret was the last person in England who knew how to make it properly. He loved the comforting smell of the dish baking in the oven and the coziness of the experience of eating it. When he was eating shepherd's pie, West had a sense of well-being, particularly when he washed it down with Bulmer's cider. To him, English cider was the best, better than French or Irish, but they were in fashion now. It irked him when the advertisements for French and Irish cider described them as "original cider," as if English cider had somehow been an imitation.

At the table, West helped himself to a giant portion and poured the cider from the long bottle into a squat glass.

"If she didn't lie, "Margaret interrogated, "I'll bet she gave you the runaround."

She ate slowly and solemnly, chewing her food like a cow. West liked the way she ate; it enhanced the domesticity of his environment, which he valued above all else. He despised glamour. Princess Diana had made him uneasy. To him, royalty was not about glamour. "If you understand royalty," he would say, "you know it's the opposite of glamour. It's about identification with the people. The Queen is the head of the family. We're all part of a family in England." He defended the Queen when anyone accused her of being dowdy. No, Diana was not what royalty was supposed to be about. She had been too showy and entirely too glittering. She was more Hollywood than Buckingham Palace. While he didn't entirely approve of Charles, he found him more suitable, if dense. The one he liked best was William, who had the kind of charisma that arose out of a true popular loyalty and identification. William was the ideal young Englishman, handsome, athletic, and down to earth.

"To the contrary," West explained, not altogether accurately, "she was quite helpful, actually."

"You've got a lead, then?"

"Not exactly," he said. "More like an explanation. She said Singh's killers didn't act alone. Someone put them up to it."

Margaret hummed to herself. "A likely story," she smirked.

She cleared away the plates and brought a gooseberry trifle out for dessert. Without mounds of sugar, gooseberries were so tart they made your lips pucker so tightly they formed a figure eight. West polished off a substantial amount and folded his hands on the rise of his stomach.

"Her name is Molly Stock. Poor thing. She wants to be tough but I think she's faking it. All that talk about Hitler. I've got to break that façade. She'll talk, you'll see."

"I don't like any of it," Margaret confided. "How did it all come to this? Race riots, hoodlums, Nazis, foreigners everywhere. It's not that I didn't like Singh. I did. And his wife. But there are too many of them, Stanley, you've got to acknowledge that. We can't take them all in, it simply isn't possible."

While absorbing Margaret's tirade, West pulled the folded article out of his pocket. He examined the photograph of Montague Rogerson and thought for a moment. It reminded him of someone else. The face was an older version of Michael Rogerson.

"I'll be a monkey's uncle," he declared.

"You'll be a what?" Margaret looked up from her dessert plate in astonishment.

"A monkey's uncle," he repeated.

"Stanley," Margaret laughed. "I haven't heard that expression in at least ten years."

"All the same," West narrowed his eyes. "All the same." He put the article back in his pocket.

With their evening meal over, West and Margaret retired to watch television. It was a documentary on Hampton Court, produced and narrated by Prince Edward.

"Doesn't he make enough money being a royal?" Margaret complained. "Does the BBC have to pay him also? I mean, that's us paying him twice."

Edward rambled on about Wolsey and Henry VIII as he strolled around the grounds. He was dressed in a houndstooth jacket, cavalry twills and a maroon turtleneck.

"Do you think he's queer?" Margaret wondered aloud.

"Dunno," West mused. "How would I know? I mean, there's only one way to know."

"I don't think I could fancy a queer king," she pondered.

"No one is asking you to," West quipped, patting her on the knee.

"Oh Stanley, you are a card," she chuckled. "Would you like a tumble?"

West raised his eyebrows in mock astonishment.

The ring of the telephone interrupted them. It was Doli Singh.

"Stanley, it is Doli. Another dreadful thing has happened."

West felt remiss. He had phoned but had not gone over to see her in several days.

"What is it?"

"A car pulled up. Someone threw a brick through a window with a note tied to it. It was clipped-out letters from the newspaper. It says, "Tell the nigger-lover West he's next.""

The next morning, West stopped by Doli Singh's to pick up the note and then hurried to Detective Chief Inspector Guilford "Gilly" Morrison's office. In theory, he had a Superintendent above him, but his relations with Morrison were such that he had easy access to him.

"Come in, West!" he heard Morrison shout in a clipped, military British accent. Morrison was perfectly English in every respect except for the fact that he was black. His parents had emigrated to the U.K. from Barbados and he had worked his way up in the Cambridge police department after taking a degree in criminology at the University of Hull and serving for several years in the military with the rank of sergeant.

Morrison had a genial sort of charisma associated with the British army and exuded self-confidence. He was a short, well-built man with a shiny, bald black dome of a head and a smart, neatly trimmed moustache.

"I say, West, you look distraught," he remarked, as he extended his hand to greet him.

"I've been bloody threatened," West replied, handing Morrison the note. "Some clown hurled this through a window of Doli Singh's house."

Morrison perused it with his dark penetrating eyes.

"Not unusual, really," he said. "I doubt it's from the same people who did in Singh. All the same, we'll look into it. Is it all right if I keep this?"

"I'd like a copy," West requested. "And by the way, did you know that the vet, Michael Rogerson, has a brother who is a well-known psychiatrist?"

"Still on that business of Prince Charles's polo pony? I should think that the Singh business would be a top priority. We've got no evidence on Rogerson. It was an accident. If I were you, I would let it go."

"If Rogerson were dealing drugs, it would be a different matter, wouldn't it?"

"But who says he is?"

"He's got some clients with expensive dogs."

Morrison grinned. "I expect so. Do you suspect the dogs of foul play?"

"They pay him a ton of money, far above the going rate. I phoned up his office and used an assumed name. I said I had a sick Alsatian. The girl at the phone put me on to Rogerson's assistant, who told me what it would cost. Two hundred quid for the first visit, and that's before any treatment. He said Rogerson would need to interview me to get the dog's medical history as well as my own. Why would he need my medical history?"

Morrison shrugged. "Maybe he wants to know if you're well enough to take care of an animal. Have you had a heart attack, that sort of thing. It's rather imaginative, come to think of it. I expect there will be an article in *The Times* on the swank vet who cares about the animals he treats as well as their masters. 'Dr. Rogerson, what is the significance of asking a dog owner about the owner's health?' 'A good question. Obviously, I don't treat the owners. I'm a vet, not a physician. But I know from experience that animals reflect the condition of their masters. Dogs, particularly, are sentient beings. If the owner is, say, depressed, this might lead to neglect, even if it is inadvertent.'"

West narrowed his eyes. "The part he would leave out is when he asks the owner if she's taking anything for her depression. She says no, and he then gives her some medication for the dog. 'Be careful not to take any of this yourself. It's a relaxant. It will make you very drowsy. But come to think of it, you might want to consult someone who could prescribe something for your depression and to relax you.' The vet who cares, precisely."

Morrison looked at the note again and put it face down

into the copier. He stuck a piece of paper in and waited for
the copy to emerge.

"You still think he drugged the horse?"

"If Manuel Bugatz paid him to do it, why not?"

"You don't think too highly of Michael Rogerson, then?"
Morrison said, handing West the copy.

"I think he's a slimy little shit," West answered.

"We'll keep someone outside your house for now," said
Morrison. "Any leads on Singh, then?"

"There's a girl. She might know something."

"Name?"

"Molly Stock. Some sort of neo-Nazi."

Morrison rolled his eyes. "From central casting?"

"You might say that," West said.

"Jolly good," Morrison concluded. He must have been the
last person in England to use that expression. He told West he
was getting ready to go to Lords for the test match against
Pakistan but would start an investigation into the note.

"You look a bit tired, West. Try to get some rest," he
advised.

By the time Morrison got to Lords, the riot was in full force.
Earlier, a Pakistani student had defaced the statue of cricket
immortal W. O. Grace at the entrance to Lords by spraying
"Racists!" on it with red paint. The British National Party
immediately mobilized an army of supporters to harass Pakistani
cricket fans who had gathered to support the Pakistani team.
A BNP speaker exhorted the crowd to "Send the Asians back
where they came from," and was hit by a flying egg.

"We are not from somewhere else!" someone shouted. "We
are from here!"

The police had been unable to restrain the hostile camps,
which converged on each other with cricket bats and clubs.
Confronted with the mayhem, Morrison beat a hasty retreat,
narrowly escaping a blow to the head. As a group of thugs
converged on him, he flashed his police badge and they backed

off. "It's a nigger bobby!" one of them screamed, making an obscene gesture. Observing the police increasingly losing control, Morrison joined them in trying to subdue the mob. The riot police finally arrived, sirens blaring, and the rioters began to disperse to avoid arrest.

"A lovely day at Lords," Morrison quipped to a constable, dusting himself off as he headed towards a patch in Lord's Tavern where a contingent from MI5 had gathered.

All was decorum, as the English and Pakistani teams, resplendent in whites, bowled and batted to polite applause. Pakistan crushed England in a one-sided match by seven wickets.

"So strange," Morrison observed to a spectator. "Rioting outside and old England inside."

"Not really," the codger barked. "Civilization is always precarious. You never know when it will all fall apart. Never take anything for granted, I always say. Someone could bomb Lords tomorrow, terrorists, the IRA, who the bloody hell knows. At least these Pakistanis know how to play cricket. They learned it from us, of course, but they would never admit it."

Suddenly, he realized to whom he was speaking. "I make an exception for the West Indians. They've been playing cricket for almost as long as we have. *Beyond a Boundary* and all that." He was referring to C.L.R. James, a West Indian who wrote the greatest book on cricket.

"I'm not West Indian," Morrison exclaimed.

"What do you mean you're not?"

"I was born here. I'm British."

"No offense meant, old chap," he stuttered. "By all means, British."

He offered his hand in an apology and Morrison shook it politely. As he watched the old gent dodder off, he shook his head in bewilderment. In his entire life, he had been to Barbados only once, for his grandmother's funeral. The heat had been unbearable, but everyone was wearing formal suits and dresses. The black Anglican priest at St. George's Church had extolled the old lady's virtues as "a Christian, a teacher, wife, and mother." He could see the ocean from the church, the waves crashing against the rocks.

Chapter Thirteen

Sarah Filburn had contempt for most men of her class. Eton, Harrow, Winchester, Charterhouse, and Marlborough all produced the same kind of person. Dashing and Byronic for a brief period at Oxford or Cambridge, they soon lapsed into mundane and tiresome existences at merchant banks in the City. Their good looks quickly faded from over-eating and drinking and their conversation, bright and witty during their undergraduate period, became repetitive and boring. She had studied German literature at Oxford and her passion was music. Her favorite composition was the Walton violin concerto, and, for her own instrument, the Elgar cello concerto. While she never believed she would define her existence through a man, she was a passionately sexual being, for whom physical contact gave her not only immense pleasure but deep metaphysical meaning. She was statuesque and athletic and moved with the predatory grace of a tigress.

She was briefly engaged to a banker from Winchester and Balliol with a temporarily exquisite body. Their life together was a social whirl of glittering parties in London and lavish weekends at country houses, at which she sometimes gave informal concerts in a low-cut evening gown that revealed a considerable amount of cleavage.

It was at the country home of self-made industrialist Teddy Ranier in Devon, while she was playing Bach's Suite No. 4 for Unaccompanied Cello, that she looked up and saw the ethereal blond man staring at her with his languid and romantic eyes. He was wearing white flannel trousers, a double-breasted blue blazer, an open striped shirt, and a florid ascot. She smiled briefly and then continued playing, her dark brown hair falling partly on her face.

After the applause, he got up and walked over to her, offering to get her a glass of champagne. She accepted his offer and they sat down together, while her fiancé engaged Ranier in earnest conversation about the American stock market.

"I find the cello suites very romantic," he observed. "Most people don't think of Bach as romantic, but he is."

"To me, Bach is the Baroque," she demurred.

"But isn't it a mistake to categorize by era?"

His voice was hypnotic, very soft and sensuous. "It's the same for people. Ask any one in England and they'll tell you Germans are all engineers without soul. But it's untrue. We are the real romantics, particularly the Bavarians. I am Bavarian. When I listen to Bach, I become almost primitive, particularly on warm summer nights like this."

Sarah looked over at her fiancé with Teddy Ranier, all artificial enthusiasm and concern. She felt only disgust. She switched her conversation with von Oberman from English to German. "I detest my fiancé," she confided.

"Would you like to walk outside?" he suggested. "I think it would be pleasant."

They meandered down a path leading to a gazebo.

"This is charming, don't you think?" he smiled.

"Very." She wanted him. She wanted his hands on her breasts as he entered her.

He opened the door to the gazebo and led her inside. She felt his hands holding her tightly on her back, pressing her against him. He was erect. She led him to a sofa and pulled him onto it.

"I am a cello. Play Bach on me," she whispered.

Von Oberman continued to keep his appointments with Montague Rogerson after the latter agreed to serve as honorary chairman of the St. John Earp Society. He cautiously led Rogerson to believe that he was getting more pleasure out of being a man.

"The more you understand your relationship with your mother, the more you will be able to establish your sexual identity," Rogerson confided. The opium had given him a height-ened sense of awareness and increased energy.

"Earp is helping me, too," von Oberman nodded. "His art is masculine yet sensitive. It is wrong to identify the sensitive only with the feminine."

Rogerson glanced at his watch.

"Are we near the end for today?" von Oberman asked.

"A very good session, I should think," Rogerson responded.

As von Oberman wrote out a check, he casually suggested it might be a good idea to get Prince Charles involved in the Earp revival.

"Why Prince Charles?"

"Think of the publicity. It would turn things around overnight," von Oberman said.

"It might do more harm than good," Rogerson mused. "He's a national joke."

"All the same, he is the Prince of Wales. He makes news. You remember what Wilde said? There is no such thing as a bad public notice."

Rogerson paused. "Do you own any Earps?"

"Actually, yes," von Oberman confessed.

"Then, if Earp becomes fashionable, they will be worth more," Rogerson concluded.

Von Oberman laughed. "Surely you don't think this is my motivation?"

"Think of Berenson. Think of Clement Greenberg. They both did it."

Greenberg had collected Jackson Pollock and promoted him through his criticism, temporarily transforming the mean-ing of art from beauty to the sublime. In the process, he man-aged to become rich. Before becoming an art critic he had sold neckties. Berenson used his criticism to inflate the value of the art he acquired while wandering around Europe. Rogerson was convinced that von Oberman was cut from the same cloth. Had he been suckered in with this Earp business? He had done it as a favor, having become attached to von Oberman, without allowing himself to become excessively affectionate. In this respect, he was still a Freudian and eschewed the closeness avowed by Ferenczi, whose "kissing therapy" had so offended the master. He had seen no harm in it, and besides, he did have a strange affinity for Earp's work. There was, he convinced himself, no real harm in what von Oberman was doing. But Prince Charles? The irony was incredible. He couldn't wait to tell Marbury.

When Rogerson phoned him, Marbury was in a state of agitation.

"Have you learned of the Queen's Birthday Honors for 2001?" he panted. "An Order of the British Empire for Jane Birkin, for running around naked in *Blow Up.* Do you remember that film? Directed by that degenerate wop, Antonioni. Oh yes, she moaned as though she were getting fucked by a horse in that stupid song, *Je t'aime (moi non plus),* which she recorded with her Frog lover. Get this. She is being honored for her services to acting and British-French cultural relations. What a joke! Screwing Serge Gainesbourg is her contribution to British-French cultural relations. Acting? This is hardly Dame Judith Anderson. This could happen only under Tony Blair."

Rogerson was dumbfounded that Marbury was not on the list. Undoubtedly Marbury was as well. "Something fascinating has happened," Rogerson managed.

"Of course it has. Britain has been turned into a garbage dump. Positively fascinating. Do you know anything else, by any chance?"

"Actually, yes," Rogerson interjected. "But I think it best if I told you in person."

Rogerson dashed over to Marbury's chambers in the Inner Temple. Marbury's wig and gown were thrown on a chair, and he was sitting with a large whiskey below a portrait of Mansfield.

"Sorry about the knighthood, Philip," Rogerson offered.

"Not to worry, Monty. I plan to be photographed running

about Hyde Park in the nude with my wig on. That should do it. So what have you got?"

"Do you remember that fellow who came over to us at the Tate Modern? Christian von Oberman? He is actually my patient. He's the one who got me to be the honorary chairman of the St. John Earp Society."

"Dreadful artist. I wondered why you did such a thing."

"I thought it might boost his confidence if he thought I approved of Earp. Also, I don't quite agree with you. I think Earp is important. But that's neither here nor there. What is fascinating is that von Oberman says he wants to get Prince Charles involved in his efforts to promote Earp's work."

"Does he know him?"

"No. But his fiancée does."

"Lady Sarah Filburn?"

"Right."

Lady Sarah Filburn had started taking art history courses in London at the Sotheby's Institute of Art. Having decided against a career as a concert cellist because of the constant comparisons with Jacqueline Dupree, she planned to work for Sotheby's and then open her own gallery, first in London and then in New York. Charles Saatchi encouraged her and introduced her to Larry Gogosian, who offered her a job. "Watch out, Larry," she told him, "I'm going into business for myself." Gogosian had started out selling concert posters after college, parlaying this into a career that had earned him fortunes. He had made Eric Fischl rich, even if Fischl's paintings were not selling for as much as they had a number of years ago. The trick was to find an artist, make him hot, and cash in. She saw herself teaming up with von Oberman, whose family had suffered some serious financial setbacks as the result of a speculative real estate deal in Atlanta, Georgia.

Von Oberman had confided in her that he needed to make more money than he was earning at the Courtauld Institute and through his private consultations authenticating paintings. Filburn's own family was land poor, British aristocrats with a manor house in Yorkshire listed in the National Register, but little else except contempt for anyone who worked for a living. When she learned that New York art dealer Mary Boone had said that "selling paintings was like selling hamburgers" and that John McEnroe was now making big money selling art, Filburn knew she had found her calling. She would describe her meeting with von Oberman as "serendipitous" and was determined to enter into a personal and business partnership with him. Rich Germans bought art as a defense mechanism against accusations that they were boors, and von Oberman would have access to this exquisite market. Since she spoke German fluently, she could convert this asset into sales. With his credentials as an art authenticator as well as an accomplished connoisseur of fine art, no one would question his judgment as to a work of art's authenticity or its value. With her social caché, she would have London and New York eating out of her hand.

If she found von Oberman sexually ambivalent, which she did, this did not deter her. It was in fact she who had suggested that he approach Prince Charles, or so she believed. He had put the idea into her mind so subtly she was fully convinced she had conceived of it. What he had not confided in her was his other occupation, with which he handsomely supplemented his income: hired assassin working for the Muller Group, with the codename of Ramos. The *Abwehr* and the Muller Group had trained him. He was a master of disguise who could shift from one identity to another in seconds, the Bavarian prince, the Swedish bombshell, the dark, transsexual seductress.

It was these identities that enabled him to cope with the multiple-personality disorder from which he suffered. How authentic was his desire to be a woman? He was not even sure of that himself, although he knew it had something to do with the masochism of his nature. But he didn't kill just for the money. It was something that gave him a special kind of pleasure and allowed him to express the sadistic side of his personality. Killing as a woman balanced out his suffering as a woman. In reality, he had no idea who Christian von Oberman really was. But he had not gone to Montague Rogerson to solve his psychological problems. He had done so to get to Prince Charles, without Sarah Filburn doing it directly. Rogerson was well connected and would be the perfect foil.

Marbury seemed somewhat reserved to Rogerson. He said that Harrington was now throwing all of his energies into "The Bà," and was convinced the time was not ripe for anything dramatic. Lamont-Hope and Waterloo agreed, he assured Rogerson.

"But if Charles could see that things were turning, that Blair will not last long and that the Tories were going to stage a comeback, he might change his tune and fall into line," Marbury argued. "In which case, he would be more valuable alive than dead."

"What are you suggesting, Philip?"

"By all means, get him involved with St. John Earp. Work on him to see the error of his ways. You're the perfect chap to do it. You're a psychiatrist."

"But how?"

"Present him with an Earp as a gift of the Society. Something of the sort. Lots of fanfare, the lot. He will lap it up, I promise you."

"You think?"

"Absolutely."

Rogerson was pleased with this possibility. He despised Charles and welcomed the opportunity of getting inside his head to change his direction. If he handled it properly, he might even snare Charles as a patient. The possibility entranced him. He would get von Oberman to donate a lesser Earp for the gift. Charles would never turn it down. Or Charles might even buy one. All the flattery would induce him to join the Society as a patron. The idea of the importance of English art as the custodian of tradition was something Charles would buy into, given his views on architecture. And Earp was nothing if not

a traditionalist, albeit a bizarre one. If Charles were conservative in art and architecture, couldn't he be made to see that
this should lead him to conservatism in politics? Rogerson
believed that Charles was a cipher and subject to the influence
of others. He would save Charles from his own wrong-head-
edness, just as he was saving Christian von Oberman from his
fantasies. Instead of killing one prince and saving another, he
would save them both.

"Very well," Rogerson asserted. "I'll work on it."

"You do that," Marbury smiled. "But you must excuse me.
I haven't even offered you a drink."

When West phoned Sheila Robinson at New Scotland Yard to
tell her his life had been threatened following Singh's murder,
she paused and then remarked: "They'll never kill a cop."

"Will you admit you said that after they blow up my house?"

"You're being melodramatic, Detective Inspector West.
We're experiencing racial violence everywhere now, and we're
coordinating all the investigations. But the Singh murder was
an isolated incident. It should come as no surprise that they
have threatened you. They are small-time thugs feeling their
oats."

West was becoming increasingly furious, but he suppressed
his rage.

"They're all on drugs. Someone is supplying them and I
think it's Michael Rogerson."

West could sense Robinson's sneer on the other end of the
phone.

"Another of your hunches, West? But we'll tell DRVIU to
have a look, and we'll examine the threatening note for clues.
And, of course, we're looking into Singh ourselves. But keep
this quiet, would you? This has been bad for Cambridge's
image. We don't need to damage it further if it can be avoided."

West didn't reply. At least he had obliged them to do something. Apathy and indecision were, he believed, the two tragic
flaws of his countrymen. How great an emergency did it take

to get them to act?

"Did you know," he finally asked, "that Michael Rogerson's brother is head of some society for an artist named St. John Earp?"

"Never heard of him. Who is his brother?"

"Dr. Montague Rogerson, a shrink."

"Nothing unusual about that, is there?"

"Dunno, really. This whole bloody cast of characters is giving me the creeps. But thanks all the same."

"Keep in touch," Robinson suggested, and hung up.

West checked his e-mails. There was one from Molly Stock. It was only one word: "Smack."

West knew immediately what it meant and e-mailed her back to meet him at The Dragon at nine o'clock that evening. The very existence of Molly upset his equilibrium, with her nihilistic leather jacket and her boots. Like Morrison, he was becoming increasingly perplexed by the growing contradictions in English society. This year's men's finals at the All England Club at Wimbledon had been the most exquisite in the tournament's history, a testament to British civility and sportsmanship. Ivanisevic and Rafter had played magnificently, both keenly aware of the history of the last great tennis event on grass. By holding onto the great tradition of lawn tennis, England stood its ground against the encroachments of mass culture and technology that undermined the traditional rituals which were the glue of an organic civilization in which people cared for each other.

But the day before Ivanisevic managed to win the final in five sets after three days of postponements, white and Asian rioters in Bradford used bricks, bats, hammers, fireworks and firebombs against the police and local businesses. Rumors had spread that the white supremacist National Front was going to defy a government order and stage a march, leading the Anti-Nazi League to stage a counter demonstration. As the violence spread to the Asian area, rioters firebombed a Labor Party social club and looted and burned down a BMW dealership. How long, West wondered, could the great and good of England withstand the growing violence and hatred?

Molly quickly e-mailed him back that she would be there.

West had dinner and watched the news on television before heading over to The Dragon. Greece announced its first confirmed case of mad cow disease. Because of the ineptitude of some ill-informed British civil servants, suppliers had been allowed to dump cattle feed made from offal on the market, which contaminated the cows. British beef, once the stuff of legend, was now feared both at home and abroad; even the Wests had given up on it. He remembered his one visit to Simpsons-on-the-Strand, with the waiters wheeling around the carts with magnificent cuts of juicy roast beef on them, and slicing and serving the meat at the diners' table. You'd be insane to eat that stuff now, he thought to himself. And the disease continued to spread.

The newscaster went on to say that the foot and mouth disease scare was abating and that it was now safe to go walking in many parts of the countryside. But what she omitted was that countless small farmers had gone belly up and that British agriculture as it had been practiced for centuries was rapidly coming to an end. Rural England was being transformed. The small farmers who had fed Britain and given it her stability were giving up, leaving the industry to agribusiness. A whole way of life that was the heart of Tory Britain was vanishing before West's eyes.

As he expected, The Dragon was packed and Molly was already at the bar, puffing on a fag. She seemed nervous.

"They should change the name of this pub to The Foot and Mouth or The Mad Cow, because it's so fucking diseased," she quipped sardonically, "like the rest of this fucking country."

"Can we dispense with the insults?" West cut her off. "What do you mean 'smack?'"

"You know what I fucking mean."

"You tell me."

"If I did that, you'd haul me off to fucking jail."

"I told you I wouldn't do that. As long as you tell me what's going on.

"Why don't you just give me immunity?"

West looked at her. She was sweating and her eyes were red.

"Because it would get out. I can't afford to tip anyone off. Yet. Besides, you haven't done anything illegal that I know of. You didn't kill Singh and you haven't been selling drugs."

"Suppose I was buying them?"

"Are you?" West questioned.

"What if I fucking was? What I can tell you is that the money is gone."

West's suspicions were confirmed. "You used it for smack," he asserted.

"What the bloody hell do you fink I used it for? Tea and crumpets?"

Molly chain-smoked throughout her tirade. "I need more fucking money," she demanded.

"I'll get it for you. Who sells you the drugs and who killed Singh?"

"Look," she sneered, "if you want horse, you go to a fucking horse-doctor, right? Did Singh ever tell you that he had a nephew who died of an overdose? I'll bet not. He was a sanctimonious wog. It's not just the whites who are fucking up, get it? The fucking wogs never go to the police when one of them does drugs. It might hurt somebody's chances to get into Bristol. No wonder he got his head bashed in. He was looking to blackmail the pusher."

"The pusher. It's Rogerson."

She didn't answer. West pulled out his wallet and handed her five twenty-pound notes. She grabbed them, gulped down her rum and Coke, and looked around the pub.

"The killers? It could have been Robby Snodgrasss over there, the guy with the red hair and the baggy trousers. I'm not sayin' he actually done it, because it was a bunch of 'em.

But Robby is paid to do stuff like that."

Before West could ask her another question, she darted out of the pub. Snodgrass was looking daggers at him. He got up from his table and walked menacingly up to West.

"So the copper is fucking Molly Stock. What about that?"

"What are you talking about?"

"I saw you give her money. Molly fucks for money. You know that. Was that a payment in advance to have her tie you up and whip you? I'll bet it was. Oh, Molly is good, really good. She's the bloody best. Some of the most important dons in Cambridge are her clients. There's a guy at King's she pisses on, and another one at St. John's she beats to a bloody pulp before she rapes him."

"What do you know about Singh?"

"You mean the bloody wog who got his head stomped? You've got to be joking. If, and I say if, I knew anyfing about that, I wouldn't be telling you, would I?"

West sipped his pint. "I expect not," he answered.

"If you're ever short of cash," Snodgrass grinned, "I'm your man. If you know what I mean."

"I could arrest you for bribing a police officer," West shot back.

"But you wouldn't fucking do that, would you? It's your word against mine, right? But like I said, I'm always here. You know where to find me."

Robby Snodgrass wasn't a pusher himself. But he got people money to buy drugs and charged. Half the people in The Dragon owed him money. If they didn't pay, he taught them a lesson they wouldn't forget. Invariably, they found the cash. The beating of the president of the Cambridge Union, which went unsolved, was mistakenly attributed to rightwing racist extremists. The undergraduate from St. Catherine's College said he didn't recognize his assailants.

West trusted Gilly Morrison but was frustrated by the lack of results. He had to keep after Molly. If she owed money to Snodgrass and couldn't raise enough hooking, she would come to him. But he couldn't afford to give her any more. Not without Margaret getting wind of it. And now that he knew things about Singh he had never suspected, his righteous indignation was starting to fade. He needed to talk to Doli Singh.

The caller told Philip Marbury that he was to meet the "operative," as the voice on the phone described him. The voice was deep, with a distinct eastern-European accent. There was a house in Bayswater, but he would not be told the address. He would be picked up in a black Mercedes and driven to it, blindfolded. The voice told Marbury that the money had been transferred as agreed and the time was approaching for the contract to be fulfilled. "We are a service company," the voice explained, "and customer satisfaction is our objective. Otherwise, we could not stay in business."

Marbury put down the phone and poured himself a drink. Things were moving along. Michael Portillo had acknowledged homosexual acts while at Cambridge, an excellent ploy for a Tory in Blair's Britain. Margaret Thatcher had denounced him as "that Spaniard," which was perfect. Everyone hated Thatcher now, and guilt over treatment of immigrants was becoming the national pastime. Portillo's parents *were* immigrants. If only the rest of the Conservative party weren't such dunces. Formerly Thatcher's fire-breathing defense minister, Portillo had made himself over. Now he was able not only to distance himself from her, but also create the impression that she was his worst enemy. With Charles out of the way and William the next in line to the throne, the mood in the country would change and Blair would be thrown out. "They are not long, the days of wine and roses," Marbury quoted from Dowson, "so we'd better be at it."

The car arrived on schedule at eleven o'clock at night. Marbury got in the back seat and a stylish woman with short dark hair blindfolded him. He had caught a glimpse only of the back of the driver's head, white and bald. They drove in silence for about twenty minutes and came to a stop.

"I'll take the blindfold off once we're inside," she told him, and led him up the stairs to the front door. She rang and a tall man in a black turtleneck and trousers let them in. Still blindfolded, he entered a lift that took them up to the top floor. While they were going up, she removed his blindfold. The woman, tall and dark, was stunning. She wore designer sunglasses.

"This way, Mr. Marbury." She pointed to a closed door and opened it, standing aside to let him go in first. She followed him into the room, which was empty except for two chairs and a standing ashtray.

"Sit down, Mr. Marbury," she instructed.

Marbury took a chair and she sat down opposite him.

"Smoke?" she asked.

"Please."

She handed him the pack and he removed a cigarette. Then she whipped out a silver-plated lighter and engendered the flame. He leaned over, lit his cigarette, and relaxed. There was silence. Finally, she spoke in a husky voice:

"You've manipulated Rogerson well. You've met Christian von Oberman?"

"Briefly."

"He's the one who will do it."

"But I was to meet the operative here, tonight."

She smiled. "But my dear Mr. Marbury, you just have."

Chapter Fourteen

Sheila Robinson phoned West to tell him that one of Michael Rogerson's London clients, the owner of a Norwegian elkhound, had died of a heroin overdose in her townhouse in Chelsea. West restrained himself from saying "I told you so." But his vindication was undermined by the knowledge that he would have to confront Doli Singh. What Molly Stock had told him rang true, and his instincts led him to believe that Singh was up to more than even she had suggested.

"We need to know more on your end," she told him. "I'm coming out to Cambridge tomorrow. We can go and see Rogerson at his Cambridge lab together. DRVIU is conducting its own investigation, but I'm liaison to it."

West arranged to meet her at the train station at ten-thirty the next morning. He informed Gilly Morrison of developments and then proceeded to the Jewel of India on Fitzwilliam Street, an establishment that had been closed down at least three times for sanitary reasons because they served pigeon, captured from the roof, in lieu of chicken.

Doli Singh, in a blue sari that exposed a fleshy midriff, was waiting for him at a small table in the rear. West was not sure why, but the little red dot on her forehead irritated him. He pretended to ignore it. A solicitous Indian waiter greeted him and led him past the other tables. At one, a group of five Indians were having an animated conversation in Hindi, which to West, who didn't understand a word, gave off a conspiratorial aura.

"It is awful without Ashook," she lamented. "And you still haven't got his killers. And then that rock through the window."

The waiter hovered over them. "Would you care for something to drink, sir, madam?" he asked in a servile manner that somehow did not seem quite sincere.

"A sweet lassi," Doli ordered. "Stanley?"

West ordered an Indian beer, an Eagle, passing up the jumbo Taj Mahal. The waiter handed them menus and took several steps backwards. At the table next to theirs, a grey-haired, academic-looking woman in a frumpy brown dress was speaking rapidly about Paul Valéry to a thin, much-younger man in wire-framed glasses, who looked like a Ph.D. candidate. "It has always been unfathomable to me how Valéry could have been anti-Drefusard," she lectured as he nodded in agreement.

West and Doli scrutinized the menus. "Sir, madam," the waiter stepped forward, "You wish to order?"

They ordered samosas to start. Doli chose a vegetarian biryani, and West the chicken dansak.

"You know," she explained, "dansak is Parsi. The Parsis cook lentils with everything." She proceeded to describe Parsi funerals, which involved dumping the corpse outside to let the vultures peck away at the flesh until nothing was left but the bones. "It is very hard to do this now in Calcutta in a modern apartment complex. There are always a great many objections."

"I'm sure there would be," West concurred. "Of course, there would be objections in Newcastle. And there are, I'm sure."

"Stanley, what is going on?" she shifted gears.

"I was hoping you would tell me," he answered.

Doli paused and then wiped a tear from her eye with her napkin.

"This has been a terrible ordeal. Ashook was a very good person, you surely understand. This was an act of gratuitous violence."

West looked at her quizzically, then asked about the nephew and the drug overdose. Doli was taken aback and gulped her lassi instead of sipping it. At first, she attempted to change the subject, but West persisted.

"Dr. Michael Rogerson. Did he know Dr. Michael

Rogerson?"

"Yes, of course. A patient. But why are you interrogating me?"

"Tell me about your nephew."

"Which one? Ashook and I have many nephews. I mean I have many nephews," she corrected herself.

"Did Singh know anyone named Molly Stock?"

"Goodness gracious, yes. She was a patient. She never paid him, but he kept filling her cavities."

Doli dodged and ducked until West became visibly impatient. She became increasingly distraught until she confessed that her nephew Raji had overdosed on heroin.

"He was a very good boy," she started to sob. "He was at the University of Birmingham reading chemistry. But you know how it is. He would come home and go to The Dragon. It is very easy to get drugs in Cambridge now. And the young people from our country and others, they lose their traditional values and are adrift. Yes, he died from it. Ashook was heartsick. We had no children. He loved the boy."

West wanted to know if Singh had known how his nephew got the heroin.

"There are lots of ways to get drugs," she said. "Everyone knows that."

"Doli, did Singh know that Raji got the heroin from Michael Rogerson? You've got to tell me."

"Michael Rogerson is an evil man," she responded angrily.

"Evil enough to blackmail without feeling guilty?"

"You are accusing my husband, when he is dead?" she shouted, to the astonishment of the people at the other tables.

West stood his ground. "Doli, please be quiet. Everyone is looking at you."

They both resumed eating their lunches. The waiter hurried over. "Sir, madam, is everything all right?"

"Fine," West reassured him. "Everything is fine."

"Another beer, sir?"

West nodded his assent.

"Doli, if you are concealing information regarding a crime, you would be an accessory. I would have no choice but to take you in."

"You were Ashook's best friend. I can't believe this is happening. When Raji died, the family did not report it to the police. Ashook and I and his parents thought it would be bad for the family. But Ashook knew about Rogerson, or he had heard about him. So he nosed around without reporting anything. A friend of Raji's at university told Ashook that Rogerson was the source, so Ashook decided to confront him directly. Rogerson offered him money to keep quiet, but he did it subtly.

"He suggested that Ashook go into a business venture with him, a new pizza restaurant in Cambridge he would finance. Ashook's investment would have been minimal. I don't deny he was thinking about it. He had only Raji's friend's statement, no direct proof. Rogerson denied everything, so Ashook said who was he to assume he was guilty. I told him to tell you about it, but he hesitated. You know, under Blair, there is now tuition at university and it keeps increasing. Fewer and fewer people actually even apply. Ashook was paying for Raji's sister at Nottingham because Ashook's brother has no money. He is a cook. So what Rogerson proposed made sense to Ashook."

"He should have told me," West charged.

"He finally decided that he would. That was right after your last chess game. Then they killed him. And now, they are threatening you."

The waiter came to clear their plates and asked if they wanted barfi for dessert. West and Doli declined. West picked up the bill, paid it and left a tip.

Out on the street he said to Doli: "If they killed Singh to silence him, why would they want to threaten me?"

Doli looked at him sharply. "You are the police officer, Stanley, not I. But it should be obvious that they want to frighten you off."

She got into her BMW and drove off, leaving West to ponder the implications of their conversation. He suddenly saw Robby Snodgrass and Molly shouting at each other on a corner.

"You bloody bitch!" he screamed, as passers by turned in their direction.

"I paid you almost two thousand quid," she pleaded.

"Yeah, but you owe me another thousand."

West walked over to them. Instantly, Snodgrass pretended that Molly and he were having a friendly exchange.

Snodgrass grinned. "Me and Molly was just discussing a financial transaction, right, when who should come along but her john? What about it, Molly? Don't waste an opportunity like this. Take him back to your place now," he ordered.

"We'd better go," she said.

"Good girl," Snodgrass laughed. He turned and walked away, then looking back over his shoulder, told her, "I'll see you later."

West soon found himself in Molly's flat on Maids Causeway. It was dimly lit and sparsely furnished, with a mattress on the floor as the bed. It was covered with a blanket and colored pillows.

"Play along that you're my john," she insisted. "He won't be suspicious, then."

"Just confirm for me that it's Rogerson."

She lit up a fag. "Yeah, it's him. He hangs out in The Dragon, pulls up in his Jag, all ponced up, he does. It's a big joke. He says, 'Are any of your pets in pain?' And everybody laughs. It's right under your noses and nobody notices. Who would believe it, right? I mean, you never noticed until now."

To West's astonishment, Molly was disrobing. She tossed her leather jacket on the floor and then pulled off her T-shirt. She was naked from the top up. She unbuckled her jeans and pulled them down. Her thin legs were pale white and her tiny blue panties hugged her buns so tightly they looked like two grapefruits. She kicked off her boots and let her jeans slide off entirely, shoving them to the side with her foot. All she had on were the panties and her black net stockings. Molly put her hands behind her head and stretched her elbows out so her breasts protruded. She had small patches of black hair under her armpits. She approached West like a feral beast, her teeth clenched and her eyes narrowed.

West pulled back, but she grabbed him and kissed him violently, biting his lip.

"Look," she said, "you've paid me, so this is business. I'm going to fuck you and then I won't be an informer. The money will be for this."

West wanted to leave but found that he was paralyzed. He couldn't take his eyes off Molly. He let her pull down his trousers and his briefs. She got down on her knees, her hands firmly on his buttocks and devoured his penis, her tongue working like a serpent's. Molly tortured him, holding back enough so he didn't come, then working him up again until he was moaning in ecstasy. West had lost all control. She took off her stockings and panties, revealing her tight, black pubic hair. He let her disrobe him and push him down onto the mattress, so that they were tangled in the blanket, the pillows falling in different directions. Molly reached behind her head, grabbed a condom and put it on him. She slipped under him and guided his penis into her, her legs wrapped around him. Her undulations mesmerized him and he felt as though he were drowning. It was as though he were experiencing sex for the first time. He screamed when she bit his nipple, and fell on her violently as he came.

"Detective Inspector Stanley West," she mocked. "Not exactly a routine performance in the line of duty."

"If this ever gets out, I'm ruined," he stuttered.

"It won't," she assured him, "as long as you keep paying me. It might also be a good idea if you stopped bothering Michael Rogerson, if you catch my drift. You've got a wife, right?"

"If this gets back to Margaret, I'll…"

"You'll what?"

West collected himself. "No one else was here. No one will believe you."

To the contrary, Molly was quite convinced that everyone would believe her. West had taken money out of his account, lots of money. How could he explain it? Why had he given it to her in the first place, if not to buy her favors?

"I'll go to the bloody tabloids," she smirked. "But you liked it, didn't you? What's it like fucking dear old Margaret? Like goin' at it with a hippo? You was all tight and stiff. I know the type. Once in a blue moon, wiggle, wiggle, and it's over. That's not sex. That's cold mutton. Better get goin', Stanley. Mind if I call you Stanley? It's so much more intimate than Detective Inspector."

She shoved him out the door. From a bastion of British order, he was now a desperate man. He had to replace the money. He needed to think. If he moved against Rogerson, she would go after him. But Sheila Robinson was already on his trail and he couldn't stop her.

It was, then, with a certain sense of relief that he learned from Gilly Morrison the next morning that a punter had come across Molly's dead body floating on the Cam.

"Detective Superintendent Higby would like you to check out Molly Stock's flat before you pick up Sheila Robinson," Morrison advised. "You can go with Detective Constable Riley."

Constance Higby was West's immediate superior, who, to his irritation, had been promoted over him. She was an insufferable busybody who trusted no one and who had the scent of a bloodhound. She complained to Morrison that West sidestepped her by going directly to him, but Morrison, who respected Higby, nevertheless stood by West. He regarded West as a friend as well as a colleague, and saw the police hierarchy more as a bureaucratic necessity rather than a reflection of actual merit. The pressure to promote women in the force was becoming an ultimate reality, so Morrison made sure that only the best women were elevated. When West had been bypassed, Morrison took him out for a few pints to console him. "You're the best, Stanley," he reassured him. "You work for me. I'll make sure everyone understands that." West stoically accepted his situation and soldiered on.

Bright-eyed, Northern Irish Catholic Detective Constable Joe Riley came by to fetch West for the search of the flat. He was young, big, and strong, with little imagination. But he was by no means stupid. Inside the flat, he methodically went about looking for clues, like hair or blood, and checking for finger-prints. While Riley was about his business, West saw it lying on the floor, partially covered by a pillow. His pipe. When Riley went into the bathroom, West bent down, picked it up, and stuffed it into his pocket. Riley reemerged.

"Well, I don't see much here, do you, Detective Inspector West?"

"Can't say that I do, but you never know what you might have missed," he replied.

"Must have been her boyfriend," Riley conjectured. "That's what it invariably is."

West took out his pipe and fiddled with it.

Riley grinned. "The secret to this job," he said, "is honesty and fair dealing. If you can fake that, you've got it made."

West nodded his assent and they drove to the station to pick up Sheila Robinson. She was waiting for them, her hair tied back in a bun and wearing what are generally referred to as sensible walking shoes, a plaid skirt and blazer. West opened the door for her and she got in front next to Riley, who was driving, and West got in back. She had already heard about Molly Stock.

"Tell me about the dead girl," she asked West.

"Not much to tell. She was doing drugs and hinted that her source was Michael Rogerson, but she never actually confirmed it."

"What do you mean by 'hinted?'"

Riley steered them onto Churchill Road, past the college, and toward the low cement structure that housed Michael Rogerson's lab.

West leaned forward. "She said if you wanted horse, you went to a horse doctor."

"Sounds like a clever girl."

"Not too clever," Riley interjected. "Floating face-down dead in the Cam is not the way for a clever girl to end up."

"What's the report?" Robinson asked.

"We don't have a final one yet," Riley frowned. "It could have been an accidental overdose, suicide, or murder, for all we know. But there were no signs of violence."

Riley pulled into a parking space near the side of the building and they got out. The sign read "The Doctor Michael Rogerson Veterinarian Medical Laboratories." A perky blonde receptionist greeted them and asked them to have a seat and wait for the doctor. After about five minutes, Rogerson emerged in his white coat. He affected an ebullient mood and resembled a manic woodchuck.

"Ah, Detective Inspector West, how kind of you to visit me here. And these, I presume, are your friends."

"They are Detective Superintendent Sheila Robinson of New Scotland Yard, and Detective Constable Joe Riley."

"Let me show you around," he gestured. "Follow me."

He was, he explained, heavily involved in mad cow and foot and mouth disease research and had received sizable grants from the government and private foundations. The animals in cages were his living experiments and his researchers were Cambridge scientists and graduate students.

"Present foot and mouth disease vaccines are not effective," he explained. "We're working on developing one that will be foolproof. When we get it, we will administer it to all cattle at birth, thereby effectively eliminating the disease. As it is, we have been obliged to destroy millions of cattle to halt the epidemic. We have also had to destroy millions of cattle that might have contracted mad cow disease from eating a feed made from bone meal and animal parts.

"Mad cow disease, or BSE for bovine spongiform encephalopathy, is tricky because bacteria or viruses do not cause it. The culprit is an infective prion. It is a degenerative disease that affects the central nervous system of cattle that shoots the brain full of holes, so it looks like a sponge. Eat the cattle and you can get vCJD or Variant Creutzfeld-Jacob disease, a deadly brain illness. The gruesome death starts with mood-swings, numbness, and uncontrolled body movements. Eventually the mind is destroyed, like Alzheimer's, and you die. Eighty people in Britain have already died from it. And we still don't know how long it takes to incubate. It could be as long as twenty years. Millions have been exposed. There could be as many as one hundred thousand people in Britain with the disease. No one knows, and there is no cure. You can see from this why my research here is so important and why it is imperative that I continue it."

West considered Rogerson's lecture on his own indispensability an inspired defense mechanism. He knew they didn't have enough on Rogerson to arrest him. If they brought him in for questioning, he would be even more evasive. Now, their leads were vanishing, as the bodies either lay in the ground or floated down the river. The best they could do was to hound him and try to break him, while hoping that new evidence would turn up. As for himself, West wondered if he would become a suspect in Molly's death. But so far, there was nothing to indicate that she was murdered. Did she just jump in the Cam out of despair? He thought it highly unlikely. She was too hardboiled. He was convinced that whoever killed Singh and, in all likelihood, Molly, would go for him next. The obvious answer was Robby Snodgrass. But that was, for West, too obvious. Something else was going on.

"Did you know a girl named Molly Stock?" West asked.

Rogerson appeared taken aback. "I know her, yes."

"Knew her," West reiterated. "She's dead."

Rogerson kept leading them around the lab.

"That's not possible," he asserted.

Sheila Robinson, who had been silent up to this point, butted in. "She was found floating on the Cam. She made it clear to Detective Inspector West that you provided her with drugs."

"Utter nonsense," Rogerson parried. "I dated her. That was it. I admit it. She was utterly low-class, but I found her irresistible."

"She was a prostitute," West shot back.

"That was precisely what appealed to me," Rogerson confessed. "But drugs? She may have been using them, but not in my presence. She drank heavily. And when I was with her, so did I. This is terrible news. I am utterly devastated. Look, maybe we should go to my office."

"You didn't see her last night?" West asked.

Rogerson answered quickly. "No. I was at dinner with friends until very late. They will confirm this."

The disarming effect of Rogerson's bichon frise jumping onto his lap was immediate. Even Sheila Robinson smiled. West recalled the impact of the dogs in Rogerson's waiting room. But the interrogators quickly regrouped, with West demanding that Rogerson explain his relationship with Singh's nephew, Raji.

"Singh's wife has told me that a friend of Raji said he got his drugs from you, the ones he OD'd on."

"That," Rogerson demurred, "is utter rubbish. I gave Raji some work when he was home during the vacs because Singh asked me to do it as a favor. Singh was my dentist. Raji was reading Chemistry. Raji was a nice boy, but he stole morphine from the lab. I thought of going to the police but decided against it, out of the kindness of my heart. But I was wrong. Had I acted, Raji might still be alive today. He was a chemist and knew how to convert the morphine into heroin. Morphine is the base for heroin, you know. The morphine I keep at the lab is for medicinal purposes only and is completely legal."

"And Singh," West went on, "you have no idea who killed him?"

"A pack of thugs. Things are getting ugly in Britain. I can assure you that I have zero tolerance for racial prejudice. Perhaps you should do a better job patrolling the streets. As for Singh, he was an ingrate. I offered to bring him in as a partner in my new pizza restaurant for next to nothing, but he showed not an ounce of appreciation."

"Do you know somebody named Robby Snodgrass?" West asked.

"I met him at The Dragon. Molly Stock introduced him to me as the worst man in England. Other than that, no. I expect you think it's strange that I go The Dragon. It's where I met Molly. But lots of people go slumming. For me, it's a form of comic relief."

"Your client, Sybil Fellingham, OD'd on heroin," Robinson interjected. "Quite a coincidence. We found your bill in her kitchen. Four hundred pounds is a bit stiff for treating a dog for worms. And there were four bills for four hundred pounds each."

"That was the same bill mailed four times," he snapped. "I was very considerate of Mrs. Fellingham, but business is business. The bill was also for several check-ups. Frankly, I think you ought to be more careful about your allegations."

"You have no idea where she might have got the heroin?" Robinson pressed.

"How about down the street?" he laughed. "In the middle of Hyde Park, for all I know."

Then Robinson opened her attaché case and removed two documents. One was a sworn statement by Manuel Bugatz saying that the polo pony he sold to Prince Charles was in excellent condition when he bought it from him, and that Dr. Michael Rogerson had verified this. The other was Rogerson's verification, stating that the horse was in "unusually good condition, extremely strong, and well-rested."

"Were you lying when you wrote this?" Robinson quizzed him.

"Not at all," Rogerson replied. "Accidents happen. I will swear, if necessary, that I never administered any drugs to the horse to enhance its performance. Horses can cave in on you suddenly. That is precisely what happened. I was horrified that the Prince was injured."

Rogerson left it at that. West looked over at Robinson, signaling that it was, perhaps, time to go. Before they got up, Detective Constable Riley indicated that he had one last question.

"Yes?" Rogerson inquired insouciantly.

"Dr. Rogerson, there seem to have been a lot of accidents lately, serious ones. Is this all a coincidence?"

"Drug overdoses and muggings are part of daily life in Britain now. Miss Marple wouldn't know what to make of it. Neither would Poirot, for that matter. No, it's not simply a coincidence. It's a breakdown of law and order. Am I responsible for that?"

Rogerson had shaken them off, at least for the moment. West sighed and got up.

"Thank you for your time, Dr. Rogerson," he mocked.

"Not at all, Detective Inspector West. Detective Superintendent Robinson, I believe? And Detective Constable Riley."

Rogerson shook everyone's hand and watched them leave.

"Not smoking your pipe, West?" Riley smiled.

West shot him a glance and said nothing.

Chapter Fifteen

The black Mercedes had driven her to Cambridge, directly to The Dragon. It was late and, as she expected, Molly Stock was at the bar. She walked over to her, smiled, and offered to buy her a drink. Molly accepted.

"I go both ways," Molly declared.

"Mostly, I go one way, but I have been known to go both," she answered.

She was in black, with chains, and was taller than Molly.

"I have better stuff in my car that you can smoke," she told her.

"Is that an invitation?"

"You might say that," she retorted. "An invitation to an adventure."

"I don't do this for free," Molly explained.

"It'll be worth your while. Forget the going rate."

She led Molly outside, where the car was parked. They got in the back seat, the driver separated from them by a window. She drew the black curtain across it and took out two cigarettes.

"They're opium, very mild." she said, handing Molly one.

She lit Molly's and then her own, both women taking deep drags. She started making love to Molly, who let her, taking off her leather jacket and unbuckling the belt to her jeans. She put her hand into Molly's crotch and massaged her clit, while Molly, still smoking, leaned back on the car seat and moaned.

"Do you like it?" she asked.

"Yeah, I like it. Don't stop."

She kissed Molly deeply, sticking her finger inside her. Molly began to scream. "Oh, fuck! Oh, fuck!"

When Molly came, she let herself go with complete abandon, the tall, dark-haired woman manipulating her body with

confidence and skill. Molly kept smoking until she was stoned
out of her mind.

"Do you want to shoot-up?" she asked Molly.

"Yeah, oh yeah," came the barely audible reply.

She got out the syringe, poured the powder on some alu-
minum foil, and mixed it with water, stirring it with the needle. Then she drew the smack up and tied a stocking tight
around Molly's calf. The needle entered slowly and she pressed
the fluid into her, then drew out some blood and injected it
back. Molly's eyes glassed over and she began to nod.

Pulling back the curtain and the window aside, she
instructed the driver.

"Take us to the pub on the bridge near Queens."

She looked down at Molly, who was catatonic. "We're going
for a nightcap."

It was late. She stayed in the car until she could see that
the pub was closing. When the publican had locked up and
there was no one around, she dragged Molly out of the car
and unceremoniously dumped her over the bridge. She walked
to the car and they drove off back to London. She took out
her tiny cell phone and punched in the number, waiting a few
seconds before whispering: "Michael Rogerson can stop wor-
rying."

Chapter Sixteen

Montague Rogerson opened the elegant envelope to find the handwritten note from Prince Charles's private secretary. "HRH The Prince of Wales has looked into the work of St. John Earp and has found it to be of considerable merit. His paintings draw on ancient British techniques and themes in a way that gives his art a distinct urgency. For this reason, HRH The Prince of Wales graciously accepts your invitation to serve as an honorary patron of the St. John Earp Society, with the hope that his support will widen the appreciation of an English artist of such depth and power."

The letter ended with an invitation to Rogerson from Prince Charles, through his private secretary, to have a private audience with him at his office at Buckingham Palace.

The phone rang as he was absorbing the message. It was Marbury.

"Portillo is going down," he said.

"It's not possible," Rogerson countered. "He's the one."

"The votes aren't there. He's short by one. It's Iain Duncan Smith and Ken Clarke in the runoff."

Rogerson was incredulous. "Duncan Smith is for everything we want, which is precisely why he can't win a general election. Portillo was the perfect front. Clarke is a Ted Heath clone. Tory, yes, but Low Tory. His father was a butcher. He simply won't do. Even if he wins, it won't make any difference."

Marbury coughed violently. "Baroness Thatcher is extracting her revenge. She's behind Duncan Smith now. Will it work? God knows."

Rogerson collected himself. "Well, we are hard right, Marbury, no use pretending. There's no denying that Portillo softened up. But guess what? I've been invited to have an audience with Charles. He's in with the St. John Earp Society."

"Positively splendid!" Marbury revived. "When?"

"Next Tuesday. At Buckingham Palace."

"Why not St. James's? But this is your opening, Rogerson. Ingratiate yourself. Work on him and make yourself indispensable. He's a complete cipher. He wants a role, credibility. You can give it to him. Watch him go Tory, you'll see."

Marbury was fully aware of where this was going. He would have to work Rogerson to set up Charles without him having the foggiest idea what he was up to. Montague Rogerson, in his naivety, was convinced that the assassination plot was off. Marbury knew better. And now that Portillo was out, there was a new sense of urgency. Blair must have heaved a sigh of relief when he heard the news. Duncan Smith and Clarke were no threat. Blair would be at Ten Downing Street forever. Any possibility of some sort of democratic resolution was now totally remote. The coup d'état he had envisioned was now the only hope.

He congratulated Rogerson and advised him to get Charles to go all out for Earp.

"It's precisely what he needs: an obscure and perfectly weird artist that you can convince him embodies all the virtues of England. The more you emphasize British traditions, the more he will buy into it. Keep stressing that Labor is against England, that Tony Blair hates English history. Tony Blair is a European. Tell Charles that he is our only hope in stemming the tide of a continental cultural conquest. The next thing you know, they'll be speaking French at Oxford, that sort of thing."

"I can't believe this is happening," Rogerson mused. "Must run, Philip. I've got a patient."

Christian von Oberman seemed subdued. He said he was having problems with Sarah.

"Are you reverting?" Rogerson asked.

"I don't know. I don't want to lose her."

Rogerson took out the letter.

"Tell her about this."

Von Oberman read it carefully, his lips quivering.

"This is astonishing," he finally smiled. "Sarah will be entranced. It is her dream. If we can get the right publicity, her gallery will take off. It couldn't be better. So what if I couldn't have an orgasm. This will make her forget."

Rogerson took back the letter, placing it carefully in his breast pocket.

"Why do you think you can't have orgasms with Sarah?"

"Really it is simple, Dr. Rogerson. I want her to dominate and she wants to be dominated."

"If you want this relationship to last," Rogerson advised, "I suggest you make a compromise with your psyche. Just give her what she wants and have a fantasy while you do. Imagine her on top of you."

"I'll try, Dr. Rogerson."

"That's all any of us can do, in the end. Once you accept that you can't be perfect, your life will be much easier."

"An easy life?" Von Oberman shrugged. "I believe that is not my fate."

"And my job is to make you see that it, at least, can be easier. You are a sadomasochist because you fear abandonment. But if you are indispensable to her in a positive way, she will never leave you. That is the beginning of your recovery."

A chauffeur-driven dark green Daimler pulled up in front of Rogerson's town house and whisked him off to Buckingham Palace. The royal London residence was, in actuality, a rather recent acquisition, having been the town house of the Dukes of Buckingham until well into the eighteenth century. Queen Victoria was the first sovereign to live in it, taking up residence in 1837. St. James's was simply not grand enough for her. Say what one will about the monstrous dwarf, she did have a knack for pomp.

Montague's first step across the threshold was into the Grand Hall and up the curving marble stairs of the Grand Staircase. The portraits were still set in the walls as they had been by Queen Victoria. His escort guided him into a suite with secretaries typing away on computers and assorted aides dashing about frenetically, then passed them to Charles's private office. It was not unlike entering the enclave of a CEO of a major corporation. Being the Prince of Wales was, after all, a job. A smartly dressed young man greeted them.

"Dr. Rogerson, Prince Charles is expecting you," he said in a pleasant upper-class voice. He opened the door and gestured for Rogerson to go in. A voice from inside addressed them:

"That's fine, Dempster, I'll see Dr. Rogerson alone."

Charles's voice was perfect Cambridge, slightly nasal, and imbued with a hint of irony. The prince was seated in a large leather chair, his broken leg in a cast resting on an ottoman, and his left arm in a sling. A crutch leaned against the chair. He was wearing a double-breasted grey suit and a Hawks Club tie.

"Excuse me, Dr. Rogerson, if I don't get up. This is really tiresome. A few more months in the cast, I've been told."

Rogerson stood before him and bowed. "Your Royal Highness," he managed sycophantically.

"Please do sit down, Dr. Rogerson," Charles instructed, pointing to a chair close to his. It was far more modest than the one in which he was sitting. "I hope you don't mind Buckingham Palace. I prefer St. James's, but I'm having lunch with my mother today. It's been on her calendar for weeks."

Rogerson found himself seated near to Charles, looking at the strangely incongruous features of the Windsor family. He was not really ugly, but not handsome either. He was, Rogerson thought, semi-handsome in a somewhat desultory way. Whereas William was perfect, thanks to his mother's genes, Charles was a near miss, his father's handsomeness modified by his mother's ordinariness. There was something about his countenance, owing to the protruding ears, that caused him to resemble the Alfred E. Newman of the "What, me worry?" face made famous by Mad Comics.

Charles began a rambling discourse on St. John Earp, referring to various paintings he had seen in private collections.

"I am particularly impressed by the oil on canvas, 'Ship of Diogenes,'" Charles asserted, "as well as the ballpoint pen drawing, 'Pond Dwellers.'"

Rogerson sat rigid, his hands clasped. "Yes, those are outstanding examples of his work."

"One can see how Augustus John and Wyndham Lewis clearly influenced his intellectual development," Charles lectured. "Hieronymus Bosch also figures significantly, don't you think?"

"Yes, yes, Bosch, by all means," Rogerson agreed.

"It's not an exaggeration to say that Earp is one of the most controversial artists of our age," Charles added, authoritatively. "Mind you, controversy can be a good thing, as long as it's confined to the arts."

Charles then digressed into a tirade against modern architecture as a violent severing of a country's ties with its culture and traditions.

"I am distrustful of post-modernism as well," he continued. "It is nothing more than another strategy to subvert the classical paradigm."

"Exactly," Rogerson nodded emphatically.

"Earp is controversial precisely because he goes against the tide," Charles stated. "He is an English mystic with deep roots in the ancient. He is radical in the best sense of the word. Many would disagree, but that is why the English monarchy is radical."

He was becoming somewhat agitated. "The monarchy is the only English institution that goes directly to the roots of what is mystically British. I think this is implicit in Earp's work. He is a radical, not a revolutionary."

"Exactly," Rogerson repeated. "And in all respect, Your Royal Highness, I believe this has serious implications for today's Britain."

"How so?" Charles asked.

"I believe we are in grave danger of losing our connections with the past."

Charles adjusted himself in the chair.

"I couldn't agree more. But I don't think there's an alternative to Blair, politically. But we are getting away from our purpose. I suggest we have an exhibition of Earp's work at the Fitzwilliam in Cambridge. What do you think?"

"An excellent idea, Your Royal Highness," Rogerson answered.

"Well, we'll work on that." Charles instructed. "Now, who is this Prince Christian von Oberman on your board?"

Without indicating that von Oberman was a patient, Rogerson recited his credentials to Charles.

"I look forward to meeting this fellow. Dr. Rogerson, you are a psychiatrist, I believe."

"Yes, that's right, Your Royal Highness."

Charles looked straight at him. "Would you mind if we discussed a few things before you left? In strictest confidence, of course."

Rogerson listened intently as Charles poured his heart out to him about his feelings of guilt about Diana, his love for Camilla, his adultery, and his suffering because of a remote and cold father and a mother who meant well, but whose own emotional life had been frozen into a state of isolation and detachment because of her unrequited love for her husband. He had hated Gordonstoun, his public school in Moray Firth, Scotland, with its stoic cold showers and rigorous regimes. It had been his father's school, and Charles resented that he had inflicted this torture on his son. It was, he said, as though he were being punished for something he didn't do.

"Sometimes, I look at myself," he confessed, "and don't have the foggiest idea who I am. The only thing that gives me a sense of reality is that I am a father. I adore my sons, William and Harry. But I have enormous guilt feelings about that as well because I betrayed their mother. I didn't deserve Diana and I don't deserve Camilla."

"Have you ever thought of just chucking it all?" Rogerson asked.

"Chucking it all? In what way?"

"Renouncing your title. Going it on your own. You could do it, you know. It might be the only way you could prove to yourself that you have intrinsic worth."

"Don't think I haven't thought about it," Charles sighed. "But I think it would be even more cowardly to jump ship. I don't think I have any choice but to stick it out. But maybe you're right. I just don't know. I'm convinced that if I did abdicate, my father would be greatly relieved, and probably my mother, also. I suppose that's why, in the end, I can't see myself doing it. I don't want to give them the satisfaction. But I'm taking up your valuable time. Do you think we could speak again? I would, of course, pay you. I know you're a professional."

Rogerson had studied medicine at Cambridge, where he was at Jesus and went on for training at Middlesex Hospital, receiving his M.D. after a stint in the RAMC. He had always wanted to be a psychiatrist. At Paddington Green Hospital, he studied child psychiatry under Winnicott before moving on to sexual disorders. He had developed a theory that mental health was different in different societies, and that in Britain the notion of the good-enough mother had to do with the good-enough monarch.

The monarch as role model was, he was convinced, the basis for emotional stability, and that deep in the British psyche (he was somewhat Jungian in this regard) there was a profound sense of guilt over the beheading of Charles I. He equated republicanism in Britain with nihilism. His contempt for Charles was rooted in a suspicion that the Prince of Wales wasn't up to the task. Now, his worst suspicions had been confirmed. From his vantage point, he could do one of two things: he could convince Charles to abdicate, or he could, through therapy, enable him to come to terms with his obligations. Without deciding which course to follow, he agreed to Charles's request.

Rogerson had never had any use for R. D. Laing, but he wondered now if Charles were not possessed of a completely divided self. "You know," he said conclusively, "you don't have to be the best Prince of Wales. Only a good-enough Prince of Wales."

Charles answered gravely: "For the past fifteen years I have been entirely motivated by a desperate desire to put the 'Great' back in Great Britain. Everything I have tried to do—all the projects, speeches, schemes etc.—have been with this end in mind."

Rogerson bowed and made his exit.

Chapter Seventeen

Rogerson informed Marbury of the news. "By all means, get Charles together with Christian von Oberman," Marbury suggested. "Charles is no fool, believe me. He never does anything that doesn't benefit him in some way. All the charitable work, the foundations and the trusts do one thing—they promote Charles. He pays taxes voluntarily, a brilliant ploy to diffuse anti-monarchist sentiment. What's left over is enough to support an army. But he remains, at heart, a lefty. He will like von Oberman. He is the guy who can turn him around politically. The royals are all suckers for the Germans precisely because they are Germans. It runs deeper than most people think."

But who was the Prince of Wales, who also held the title of Duke of Cornwall, and whose motto was "Ich Dien" and whose crest was the three feathers? One had to go back in time to August 1346, when Edward Prince of Wales, The Black Prince, charged into battle at Crecy at age sixteen, at the outset of The Hundred Years War. Charging at him, and completely blind, was King John of Bohemia, fighting on the side of the French.

King John was killed, and emerging as "the hero the English people" was Prince Edward, who appropriated from the fallen Bohemian king the badge of three silver feathers rising through a gold coronet of alternate crosses and fleur-de-lys, with the motto "Ich Dien" (I serve) on a dark blue ribbon beneath the coronet as the crest and motto of the Princes of Wales. Ten years later, the Black Prince, as the victor at the battle of Poitiers, captured the French king, John the Good, and brought him to Canterbury, where they worshipped at the tomb of St. Thomas together.

The title "Prince of Wales" had been created for The Black

Prince's grandfather, Edward II, Edward of Caernarfon, having been usurped from the last native Prince of Wales, Llewelyn ap Gruffydd (Llewelyn the Last). Llewelyn had declared himself Prince of Wales in his futile attempt to regain territories surrendered to the English after the death of his uncle, Llewelyn the Great. It was Llewelyn's Standard for Wales that Charles carried during visits to the Principality.

Edward did not pass the title to his son. Instead, the Black Prince, his grandson, was created Prince of Wales at the age of twelve in 1343 at Westminster, and since that time, it has been the custom for the title to be held by the eldest son of most kings and queens of England, Charles being no exception.

His Investiture as Prince of Wales took place in 1969 at Caernarfon in North Wales, where the first Prince had been born. And like the Black Prince, he was proclaimed the Duke of Cornwall and the beneficiary of the fabulously wealthy trust of the Duchy created for his support. In the centuries following the Black Prince's death, the value of the trust grew, accumulating vast assets in estates and investments, until under Charles, it made him one of the world's wealthiest men.

Interred at Canterbury in a catafalque, in the crypt of his own design, the Black Prince remains "the hero of the English people" and the model by which all other Princes of Wales are judged. But toward the end of his life, after he had subdued a rebellion at Limoges, he ordered the slaughter of three thousand of the inhabitants, including men, women, and children. It was a black deed by "The Black Prince" in the days when the English were fierce and feared, but one that Viscount Harrington considered necessary and laudable.

"If Charles had that kind of killer instinct, I wouldn't be out to get him," he confided to Marbury.

Prince Christian von Oberman of Bavaria was himself of an ancient and noble lineage going back to the twelfth century. And, for the most part, while Britain was for centuries a bloodbath, Bavaria was an oasis of calm, continuity, and civilization.

The British monarchy was continually in turmoil, with plots, killings, civil wars, and rebellions, whereas one family ruled Bavaria from 1140 until 1914, the Wittselsbachs. In fact, stability did not come to the British monarchy until it was taken over by Germans. It irked von Oberman that his people were characterized as barbarians, when the first holocaust against the Jews happened in England.

The infamous "blood libel" against the Jews, who were falsely accused of crucifying a Christian boy at Easter, began in England in 1144. The Jews were banished from England by Edward I at a time when they were living in relative tranquility in Bavaria. The only "purity" law in Bavaria was the Bavarian *Reinheitsgebot* of 1516 decreed by Herzog (Duke) Wilhelm IV that beer must contain only barley, hops, and water.

Max III Joseph introduced compulsory education in 1771, ahead of the rest of Europe and the North American colonies. Bavaria sided with Napoleon and France, winning for itself the right to be an independent kingdom under the Wittelsbach monarchs. They were enlightened (King Maximillian II introduced freedom of the press before the French forced Zola into exile for writing "*J'accuse*!"), cultured, and benevolent, if on occasion eccentric — or even, as in the case of Ludwig II, insane.

Known as the "fairytale king," Ludwig is best known for building the Neuschwanstein castle and Herrenchiemsee palace. The only scandal in the family's history was when King Ludwig I abdicated in 1848 because of complications arising from his relationship with the dancer Lola Montez.

Christian von Oberman was a Wittelsbach and came to his title through his mother's family. Following the Kaiser's defeat in World War I, Bavaria was declared a communist workers' republic during the upheavals that followed. The Bavarian royal family was forced to flee Munich when the new government told them it could not guarantee their safety. Off the public payroll, the Bavarian royals were obliged to support themselves, which they did in a variety of ways. Prince Luitpold von

Bayern became the owner of the Kaltenbach brewery. Von Oberman's family accumulated wealth through clever investments in real estate in Munich and later, after World War II, in Atlanta, Georgia.

But Christian himself, without a trust like that of the Duke of Cornwall, decided it would be a good idea if he got a job. So when a relative of his mother's came to visit him in his rooms at Magdalene College, Cambridge, and asked him if he would like to join the *Abwehr*, the German Intelligence Service, he accepted readily. His cover would be his work as an authenticator of art.

The caller explained to von Oberman that his work would be in the service of the "new Germany," which could not function in a competitive world without a steady flow of information on what other countries were doing, including its allies. "Above all, we need to know what the British are thinking and doing. We don't trust them to support a united Europe, which, of course, would be led by Germany. It is our economic engine that keeps Europe going, so it is logical that we should be the leaders."

At first von Oberman's work was fairly routine. Most of the information he gathered came from the British newspapers. But gradually, with his social credentials, he was able to insinuate himself into the inner circles of British society, which was helped immeasurably by his connections in the art world. Part of his job was to penetrate MI6 and recruit someone from the British secret service intelligence agency to pass information to him on a regular basis.

He knew if he frequented enough parties and social gatherings, he would eventually meet someone who could steer him in the right direction. Lady Sarah Filburn turned out to be exactly the right person, since her uncle, Alistair Crombie, was the deputy director of MI6. At a country weekend in Devon, where Sarah's uncle had an estate, Crombie brought along his assistant at MI6, Roger Williamson.

Von Oberman took one look at him and knew instantly

that he was gay. Williamson was earnest and slight, a shock of light-brown hair falling on his forehead. He had a refined and sensitive demeanor, a delicate bone structure and cheekbones that would have been the envy of a fashion model. He had deep, sensuous grey eyes, a perfect, straight nose, and sultry lips. It took von Oberman a very short time to seduce him. Sarah was unaware that von Oberman had stolen into Williamson's room, where he made passionate love to him for ten minutes.

"Williamson and I have become perfect chums," he confided to Sarah. "He's Winchester and Christ Church, a perfectly wonderful combination."

"I know," she responded. "Uncle Alistair can't do without him."

About a week later, after several more encounters, von Oberman gently brought up the subject of British-German relations and how it would be helpful if Williamson could keep him informed of what the British were thinking on the subject.

"Oh," Williamson said slyly, "you want me to be a spy for Germany. Christian, of course I would do anything for you."

"Not just for me," von Oberman explained, inhaling a post-coital Rothman's. "I can pay you."

"What a delightful arrangement," Williamson laughed. "I get paid to be your lover as long as I betray my country. I can't think of anything I would rather do."

Von Oberman stroked Williamson's head. "This is all for world peace, I can assure you."

"Fuck world peace," Williamson replied.

"How would one go about doing that?" von Oberman grinned.

"Exactly by what we're doing, I should think."

In due course, Williamson and von Oberman began having luncheon and drinks meetings at various restaurants and clubs in London. In the overstuffed ambiance of Mark Birely's Harry's Bar, with Peter Arno drawings hanging on the walls, von Oberman led Williamson to a small discreet table in a remote corner of the dining room.

"This place gets a slightly older crowd," von Oberman gestured. No one was paying any attention to them. After they had ordered drinks, Williamson casually placed a manila envelope on the table and excused himself to go to the men's room. Von Oberman scooped it up and put it in his compact brown leather attaché case, which he placed on the floor up against his chair. Williamson returned, brushing back his hair.

"What do you want for lunch?" von Oberman asked solicitously. "And before I forget, here are the tickets to the ballet I promised you." He handed him a business-size white envelope, which Williamson put in his inside jacket pocket.

"Let's have a look at the menu, shall we?" he said.

Von Oberman had given him five thousand pounds, money which had been passed to him by his *Abwehr* case officer, whose cover was that of cultural attache at the German embassy, as payment for various phony art-authentication assignments. This sort of rendezvous took place for several months. The documents that Williamson provided to von Oberman were classified and contained generalized accounts of British estimations of German intentions in Europe. One was more specific. It was "FYEO, C" and revealed that a higher-up in the *Abwehr* was working for the British. "C" was the head of MI6.

"I believe this is disinformation," von Oberman's case officer, who was in actuality a German general, told him. "Your little boy Williamson is leading you around by the nose. If this memo were from "C," it would have been handwritten in green ink. He is taking our money and reporting back exactly what he is doing. This is not *in Ordnung*, Herr von Oberman. You must straighten this out."

"Exactly how?" he asked.

"Get rid of him," came the answer.

"That's not exactly part of the job description."

"The job description? It is very precise. You are to do what you are told."

Von Oberman was surprised that he was not particularly

upset by this turn of events. In fact, he found himself stimulated.

"But how?"

"Give him a heart attack."

"He's a bit young for that," von Oberman countered.

"Young people die from heart attacks all the time."

It was agreed that it would be the gas pistol with the hydrocyanic acid. He gave von Oberman the instrument, which he had removed from the top drawer of his desk.

"I don't have to tell you that you will not do this in view of a dozen or so people," he laughed.

"I'm not stupid."

"No, you're not. Which is why we recruited you. Good luck."

They shook hands. When von Oberman suggested to Williamson that they next meet at the bar of the Berkeley, he was delighted. "I love that place," he confided. "The lavender-blue décor is very suggestive, don't you think? Why don't we take a room for afterwards? Assumed names, of course."

"That's not too discreet, Roger. We should go to your place."

Williamson seemed a bit uneasy. "Yes, but …"

"But what? You want me, don't you?"

"Yes. Very well."

The cab took them to Williamson's flat on Donne Place and they got out. The cab pulled away. As they walked to the door, von Oberman put his hand on Williamson's shoulder, turning him so they were facing each other. He kissed Williamson, who gently pushed him away. "Let's go inside," he whispered. As he put the key in the door, von Oberman pulled out the tiny pistol. "Roger," he said. As Williamson turned, he shot him in the face and ran. In a matter of seconds, Williamson lay on the ground, dead.

"It was a good job," the general assured him. "But you're sort of hot right now. The British are complacent, but not that complacent. MI6 must be deciding what to do with you.

Unfortunately, we must terminate you, but not 'with extreme prejudice,' to use the CIA's parlance," he laughed.

"I have expenses. My parents give me only so much money. You got me into this situation."

The general fumbled with some papers. "There are other ways to make a living, Herr von Oberman."

"Such as? Do you think I can just do art authentication and pay my bills?"

"I will put someone in touch with you. I think it will solve your problems," he replied.

Two days later, the Muller Group contacted him. They wanted to interview him for a position as an "international consultant." He agreed. His code name would be Ramos. This coincided with his cross-dressing and his growing awareness of his transsexual nature. Following a number of successful assignments, von Oberman learned that the Muller Group wanted him for the Prince of Wales assignment, code name "Trinity." His fee would be five million pounds.

MI6 finally decided what to do with von Oberman. They approached him to be an informer, on a paid basis. It was an offer he could not refuse. Unaware of any of this, Montague Rogerson continued as von Oberman's psychiatrist, listening to his endless plaints about his sexual dilemma. On one occasion von Oberman arrived with a copy of *Conundrum* by the Welsh transsexual author, Jan Morris. He read out loud to Rogerson the portion of the book dealing with Morris's surgery in Casablanca by a surgeon Morris referred to simply as "Dr. B." who had "rescued hundreds, perhaps even thousands, of transsexuals from their wandering fate."

"Having something of a relapse, then, von Oberman?" Rogerson asked.

"You might call it that. I call it facing reality."

"Still, if you think about it, the surgery is irreversible."

"Jan Morris has found contentment. Why not I?"

"I am not convinced that you are the same. You aren't planning to terminate therapy?"

Von Oberman didn't answer.

"Well then, let's continue," Rogerson said.

As soon as the session had ended and von Oberman had left, Rogerson waited outside for the green Daimler to take him to St. James's Palace for his session with Prince Charles. He found Charles in a restless state, unable to concentrate.

"I'm having difficulty sleeping," he said. "I'm having night-mares."

"Can you describe them to me?" Rogerson asked.

"In the one that keeps recurring, I am a small boy and my father keeps telling me that I am not 'up to snuff.' I run to my mother, who asks me why I am so upset. I tell her and she says that I should respect my father, and that he is only trying to get me to live up to my potential.

"I run outside and there is a big crowd of people and they are all laughing at me. 'The boy who would be king,' one of them shouts. 'Would be king. Would be king,' they keep shout-ing. And then I see a giant face. At first, I can't see who it is, but then I recognize it. It is Queen Victoria. It is just her head, with the gigantic jowls. She is wearing the crown. 'You will never be king,' she says. I ask her why. She answers, 'Because you are not a king.'

"Then I see Diana, looking very sad. She is walking along a stream, holding a book. It is Boswell's *Life of Samuel Johnson*. She looks up and says 'Johnson liked King George. Mad as a hatter, King George was more of a king than you could ever be.' I try to wake up but I can't. In my dream, I rush about saying 'I will be king. I will be king.' But everything goes silent. Then I wake up sweating. It is perfectly horrible."

Rogerson affected a look of empathy. "Why is it so impor-tant to be king?" he asked.

"Because it is my destiny," Charles said. "Right from the beginning, I was told I would be king. The whole concept of monarchy is embodied in me. But I feel terribly guilty because I know my mother must die for me to fulfill my destiny. If I die before her, William will be king. I know I resent this possibility, so I feel doubly guilty. I know that everyone wants William and they don't want me. I sometimes think that perhaps I should abdicate and be done with it. But as I told you, I always reject this idea. I will simply not go wet and wimp out."

Charles looked at his watch. "I guess our time is up," he said.

"The best thing for you to do," Rogerson advised, "is to live in the here and now, without dwelling so much on the future. Things could be worse. Look at Prince Christian von Oberman. He has no kingdom at all. He is prince of nothing. England will never be Germany. We have things that endure. And you are part of that."

Charles relaxed a bit. "Thank you, Dr. Rogerson. That is very helpful," he said.

"I can give you something to help you relax," Rogerson said.

"Medication? Not at the moment," Charles said. "I simply must tough this out."

Part Three

Chapter Eighteen

Von Oberman checked with his Swiss bank. Everything was in order. The Muller Group contacted him with his instructions: "Activate Trinity. Method at your discretion. Time is of the essence." He was equipped with several miniscule gas pistols loaded with hydrocyanic acid, his method of choice. The small hypodermic needles with cyanide were also possibilities, as was his long-range rifle that he could carry anywhere and reassemble in seconds. Or it might have to be a bomb.

He dined with Lady Sarah at Gordon Ramsey and toasted the Sarah Filburn Gallery, which she now planned to open, not in London, but in Chelsea in New York.

"We have adequate resources," he assured her.

"A rich Bavarian uncle died and you've got the money," she said.

"Something like that," he said. "Charles is behind Earp fully. As soon as the publicity starts to mount, we can sell Earps in New York as the word spreads across the Atlantic. I gather he is considering purchasing one and has borrowed it to have it hung in Highgrove House."

Highgrove House, near Tetbury, Gloucestershire, had been the private residence of the Prince of Wales since 1980. The Duchy of Cornwall bought it from the Conservative MP for Farnham, Maurice Macmillan, son of the former Prime Minister, Harold Macmillan.

"So, here's to the Sarah Filburn Gallery," he smiled, raising his Burgundy grand cru glass.

Lady Sarah's white shoulders were like monumental alabaster. He could see the contours of her breasts below the cleavage. It would be a pity to have his cock cut off, von Oberman mused. He began to see the advantages of having it both ways. Maybe he could stop identifying with *Hedgwig and the Angry Inch*. Why surgery, when the genders had blended? This was just an organ; it didn't define his gender. He wondered if his vacillations would ever end, or whether he should simply enjoy his sexual ambiguity. He decided he would continue as is, at least as long as he needed Rogerson.

She toasted him back. "How soon will you have the money?" she asked.

"I have it. I just have a few things to do," he reassured her.

"Fantastic," she said.

"Yes, it is, really."

Stanley West and Gilly Morrison left for lunch at The Eagle, a museum piece of a pub refurbished at university expense to retain some sense of authenticity in the city where most pubs now served pizza and had television sets blaring.

"I loathe Constance Higby," West complained. "How could you have done that to me?"

"Water under the bridge, Stanley. This is life in Britain today. Had I not done it, they would have sacked me."

West puffed away on his pipe. "At least they still let us smoke," he said.

Morrison lit up a Rothman's.

"So what have we got?" he asked.

"What if we're barking up the wrong tree, Gilly?"

"How'd you mean?"

"Michael Rogerson. What if I am completely wrong? What if he didn't drug the polo pony to make it look good?"

"What does Sheila Robinson think?"

"She thinks I should make up my bloody mind. He's a pusher and I will nab him eventually. But my sense is that we have something different here, something I may have overlooked."

"Detective Inspector Stanley West has overlooked something?"

West leaned over the table. "Might it not be possible that Rogerson wanted the polo pony to collapse?"

"Why on earth for?"

"Do you think Diana died in an accidental car crash?"

"To tell you the truth, not really. But who would want to do something like that?"

"Someone who wouldn't want her to marry a bloody wog," West said. "Prince William's stepfather would have been an Arab. There's a good line of communication for you, an Egyptian, whose father owned Harrod's and isn't even a subject, telling Prince William what's right and wrong in the Middle East, and Princess Diana, his mother, agreeing. No, she had to go and so did Dodi Fayed. Whoever did it kept the Royals in the dark."

"MI6?" Morrison speculated. "They have reasons not to let Mohammed Al-Fayed become a subject. His brother-in-law is Adnan Khashoggi, the Saudi Arabian billionaire. They could have wanted it done."

"Not likely. But the killers have enormous influence, planting disinformation in the media to not only make it look like an accident, but to say how much everyone was grieving for Diana. If you ask me, everyone at Buckingham Palace heaved a sigh of relief. Diana and the Queen had become bitter enemies."

"And Charles is now free to marry Camilla," Morrison said.

"When the time is right, yes. 'Defender of the faith,' my foot. How can you be the defender of the faith when you are a confessed adulterer?"

"What are you driving at, West?"

"Just maybe someone now wants Charles dead, too."

"That's a bit much, West. It's almost paranoia, if you will excuse me. Rogerson is guilty of negligence. He undoubtedly used morphine to kill the polo pony's pain. The horse OD'd and crashed down on Charles, almost killing him. If that ever got out, Rogerson would be ruined. Security around Charles is incredibly tight."

"Exactly. But if it weren't negligence, it would have had to be someone they trusted."

"And if someone thought he wasn't legitimate, he would want to get rid of anything and anyone who could make him suspect," Morrison conjectured.

"Like Singh. Like Molly Stock," West shot back.

"You mean Michael Rogerson got rid of them?"

"Not by himself. He would have gotten someone else to do it."

"Who?"

"Robby Snodgrass, for one. There could be someone else."

"Any idea?" Morrison asked.

"Dunno. His brother is a famous psychiatrist, but I can't imagine he would be bumping people off."

West produced the clipping and handed it to Morrison.

As Morrison purposefully read about Montague Rogerson and the St. John Earp Society, a bullet shot from a gun with a silencer, intended for Stanley West, missed him as he bent down to pick up his pipe and ripped into Morrison's skull. He slumped over at the table, blood pouring from his head. Whoever did it had vanished.

"Oh, shit, Gilly." West jumped from his seat, pulled out a gun, and looked around the pub. "Don't anybody move," he ordered.

Morrison was dead. An ambulance and police cars arrived quickly, lights flashing and sirens blaring. Detective Constable Joe Riley questioned West, who explained that he and Morrison had been seated at the table having lunch when it happened. No, he hadn't seen anyone suspicious. Morrison's body was put on a stretcher and covered with a sheet, then carried out to the ambulance.

West was numb. Riley put his hand on his shoulder but it was no comfort. "I will find him and I will kill him," West said. "Singh, Molly, and now Morrison. This isn't England anymore."

Riley and several police constables did a sweep of the pub, as Constance Higby looked on. Her impassive look never changed. "We would appear to be in a war zone," she finally remarked. "I'll phone New Scotland Yard."

West regained his composure. "I think we had better contact MI5," he said.

Christian von Oberman quickly seduced a young German aristocrat working at the Embassy as a military attaché, whom he met at a lieder recital at the residence of the ambassador. The young man was a serious masochist, and von Oberman obliged him in his curious tastes and sexual fantasies. At von Oberman's request, he began to supply him with classified documents that von Oberman passed along to MI5. Although he demurred at first, the aristocrat accepted the money von Oberman gave him, which von Oberman, in turn, received from MI5.

They would begin their sexual rituals in von Oberman's elegant flat in St. James's Place, with von Oberman asking the question, "Is everything *in Ordnung*, Herr Domeisen?" When Domeisen answered "*in Ordnung*," von Oberman would discipline him until he shouted the code word, "Paris."

Gunther Domeisen had an insatiable capacity for pain and the more von Oberman inflicted, the more cooperative Domeisen became in supplying information. MI5 regarded von Oberman, whom they had inherited from MI6, as a valued asset and saw to it that he was protected. Their assessment of him was that he was basically a whore who would do anything for money, and until someone paid him more, they could rely on him to keep them informed on German intentions with regard to Britain and the E.U.

West, meanwhile, outlined his concerns regarding Prince Charles to Constance Higby. To his surprise, she did not dismiss them out of hand. She agreed that it might be wise to let MI5 know about his theories, at least to make certain they had left no stone unturned. She was nothing if not methodical. As Morrison's replacement as Detective Chief Inspector, she mended her fences by recommending that West be promoted to Detective Superintendent.

"I know you don't like me, West," she said. "You probably don't believe I'm here on the merits. I don't think I have to justify myself to you. I respect your ability, and we have a job to do. Gilly Morrison was the best, so we owe it to him to get on with it."

Higby's plainness was a façade. In fact, she was not unattractive in a steely sort of way. Her short-cropped brown hair and sharp features contributed to her no-nonsense persona, which was heightened by her firm breasts and her stately legs. She lived with her pet parrot in a flat in a house on Portugal Place, her personal life a complete mystery.

"We will bury Gilly Morrison with full honors," she concluded. "He certainly deserves that."

Morrison's funeral was huge. Police came from all over the U.K., Ireland, the Commonwealth, and America. They marched behind the Union Jack-draped casket, some in kilts playing bagpipes. As they made their way through the narrow streets of Cambridge, they reached the Petty Curie, where West spotted Robby Snodgrass in the crowd of onlookers. West stared right at him and Snodgrass broke into a diabolical grin. West turned his head and kept marching, but Snodgrass's sneer had been like a dagger to the heart. "This is too fucking much," he muttered to himself. "Too fucking much."

The press had universally condemned the killing of Gilly Morrison as "racially motivated," unaware that the bullet was meant for West. Socialist Worker Party militants bused in black protesters from the slums of Brixton, who shook their fists and chanted and shouted as the cortège passed by.

A fistfight broke out between some West Indians and white neo-Nazis, disrupting the funeral march and forcing the police to leave the march to subdue the rioters. The uniformed pallbearers loaded the coffin into a hearse, which sped off to the cemetery as the riot spilled over into Market Square, where it exploded into a full-fledged battle, overturning farmers' stalls and food stands.

West spied Snodgrass in the middle of it and went for him,

lunging to bring him down. But Snodgrass eluded him and tore down the street, West in pursuit. He grabbed a thug who looked like him, only to discover it was not he. West threw him aside and continued running, but Snodgrass had disappeared. Breathing heavily, with sweat pouring from his forehead, West came to a halt. He reached for a handkerchief and wiped his brow, cursing under his breath.

Detective Constable Riley was at his side.

West looked around at the mess. "Is this still England?" he asked.

"Detective Superintendent West, sir," Riley said, "I think the funeral is over."

"Not on your life," West said. "Not on your fucking life."

"It's probably time to call Robby Snodgrass in for questioning," Riley said.

West froze. How much did Snodgrass know about the money he had given Molly Stock?

"Are you all right, sir?"

"Yes, yes, Fine. Bring him in."

"Very good, sir," Riley said.

Cambridge had all but cleared out after the funeral and the riot. Snodgrass was heading for the train station when he saw the battered grey Rover. It pulled alongside him and the door swung open. A black West Indian reached for him from the back seat and grabbed him toward the car, pulling him inside. The door slammed shut and they drove off.

"What the fuck are you doin'?"

There were four of them, all with dreadlocks and small dark glasses with gold rims. The car reeked of ganja.

"We gonna cut ya balls off, mon," one of them said.

They gagged and blindfolded him and kept driving. Snodgrass did not see the giant switchblade, but he heard the sound when it snapped out of its case. His screams were muffled. After several miles along a deserted road, the door swung open again and the lifeless, bloodied body fell from the car and landed with a thud. Jimmy Cliff was singing from the tape deck: *"The harder they come, the harder they fall, one and all."*

As they got on the M1 for London, the West Indian at the wheel started speculating. He smiled, revealing one gold tooth in the middle of his otherwise perfect white teeth.

"You know da 'Black Prince,' mon?"

"Dat was da Prince a' Wales, ya know dat," the one next to him in the front seat said, taking a deep drag on the joint. "He da hero a da Hundred Years war, ya know."

"So how come dey calls him da 'Black Prince?'"

"You tell us, mon," the one in the back seat with the red, black, and green wool cap said.

"Well, I figure dey will never admit da trut. Da king was fuckin' a nigga on da side, mon, and she had dis kid, ya see. Dey kept it all a secret and no one would tell it, at all, at all. He were da oldest, so da king made him da Prince a' Wales and he would a' become da king if he'd a not died, ya see. So I figure, somewhere in Brixton, is da black heir to da trone, and he be da new 'Black Prince,' ya know."

They kept passing the joint around, each taking a slow drag. They were laughing and singing:

"The harder they come, the harder they fall, one and all."

Chapter Nineteen

Detective Superintendent Sheila Robinson informed West that she was not assigning any detective inspectors to "the Cambridge situation," as she put it, "at the moment." Sitting at her desk in New Scotland Yard, she looked at him with impenetrable blandness, the hallmark of bureaucratic self-assurance.

"The Drug Related Violence Intelligence Unit (DRVIU) has concluded that Dr. Michael Rogerson is not a drug dealer, even if Cambridge is overrun with the stuff. Singh's murder was racially motivated in our opinion, as was Morrison's. That bullet was not meant for you. While we can coordinate these investigations, there is no reason why the Cambridge police can't do the basic work. They are, after all, more familiar with the scene.

"As far as we can tell, Molly Stock was murdered by her pimp, whoever that was, and some blacks killed Robby Snodgrass after the riot at Morrison's funeral, in retaliation for his racist attitude and the belief that he was involved in Morrison's death. New Scotland Yard can and will coordinate any and all investigations, but we can't take responsibility for every municipal police force that thinks there is a revolution going on."

West glared back at her. "What about the Prince of Wales?"

"What about him? The Metropolitan Police Service, which we are, has specific national functions, among them protecting Royalty and countering terrorism in Great Britain and the DRVIU targets. The Special Branch, which is a division of the Metropolitan Police, is responsible for Royalty protection, and it has found no evidence of anything beyond an unfortunate accident at a polo game. It has given Prince Charles a stiff warning that he must be more careful and that competitive polo is something he should definitely avoid. If he is going to put himself at risk, he can't expect the police to protect him. Our own Directorate of Intelligence has six hundred trained officers in targeting, surveillance, and covert photography techniques, with the "CRIMINT" computer-based intelligence application. The Special Branch itself closely coordinates with MI5 and provides information and intelligence both for the MPS and the Security Service. If something were up, we would know about it. It's not that we don't appreciate your concerns. It's simply that we regard them, certainly at this point, as unsubstantiated."

"Then, for all intents and purposes, New Scotland Yard regards the case to be closed, as far as it's concerned?"

"That might be something of an exaggeration. If I conclude that it's necessary, in our coordination capacity, I will assign detective inspectors, and DRVIU will reconsider the matter. As for Prince Charles, that is strictly Special Branch. It's not as though I didn't take a personal interest in this, going up to Cambridge and all that. For a brief moment, I thought you might be on to something, but we have concluded otherwise. Thank you, Detective Inspector West."

"Superintendent," he corrected her.

"Ah, very good. You must be bored coming to New Scotland Yard. It's not a yard, has nothing to do with Scotland, and it certainly isn't new. Anyway, thank you. We will be in touch, I can assure you."

They shook hands and West left for his meeting at MI5.

West entered the dismal Gower Street offices of MI5, where he was shown to the office of Gwendolyn Winterton, who proved to be no more cooperative than Sheila Robinson at New Scotland Yard.

"How nice of you to come all this way for our little chat," she said. "Your concerns have been passed along to me, so here we are, then."

She spoke with an affected upper-class accent that put West

off instantly. He had no idea what her background was, but she probably didn't need this job for the money.

"I don't believe it was an accident," West said.

"Prince Charles fell off his horse and his horse fell on him. Do you ride, Mr. West?"

"No, I don't."

"Well, anyone who does, and I do, and I hate this stupid ban on fox hunting, knows that these things happen. But it's perfectly wonderful of you to keep us informed. Actually, the security of the Royals is the Special Branch's domain. Our chief function as the Security Service is to protect the nation's national security against covertly organized threats from overseas, such as terrorism, espionage, and the proliferation of weapons of mass destruction. We do provide security advice to help reduce vulnerability to threats."

"How would you describe a threat to Prince Charles?" West asked.

"It depends on what you define as a threat. Who the Prince is seeing is a matter of his private life. We're not like the FBI, poking around into President Kennedy's sex life.

"The person we call 'K,' could never be a sort of British J. Edgar Hoover. Have you any idea why we call our top person 'K?'"

"If you don't mind…"

"It's all very quaint, you know. In March 1909, the Prime Minister, Mr. Asquith, instructed the Committee of Imperial Defence to consider the dangers from German espionage to British naval ports. Six months later, following the Committee's recommendation, Captain Vernon Kell of the South Staffordshire Regiment and Captain Mansfield Cumming of the Royal Navy jointly established the Secret Service Bureau. The Admiralty required information about the Kaiser's new navy. He was determined to have a greater navy than ours, you know, so Kell and Cumming decided to divide their work. Thereafter, 'K' was responsible for counter-espionage within the British Isles, while 'C,' as Cumming came to be known, was responsible for gathering intelligence overseas. 'K' is the head of MI5, the Security Service, and 'C' is the head of MI6, the Secret Service. It all works perfectly well."

"I don't mean to be impolite," West interjected, "but I regard this as a matter of the utmost importance."

"Be assured, Mr. West," she said, "we work closely with the Special Branch and will keep your speculations, or rather, your suspicions, in mind. Has someone shown you around the building? There's a rather pleasant lunchroom, should you wish to avail yourself of it. Otherwise, I expect you have a very busy schedule and will need to be getting back to Oxford."

"Cambridge," he said.

Yes, of course. Cambridge. Do you know Professor Rosamund Nesbitt at Girton? I greatly admire her criticism of French poetry, particularly Valéry."

"I'm afraid I haven't had the pleasure." West said.

"Pity, that." She politely showed West to the door. "We will be in touch."

Chapter Twenty

"Trinity"

Trinity was the most exquisite of the Cambridge colleges. Architecturally magnificent and fantastically wealthy, its fortress-like arch that was its entrance fronted on the ebullience of Trinity Street, through which one entered into the tranquility of a small courtyard. Beyond this, through another arch, one found oneself in the midst of the grandeur of great court, with its breathtakingly impeccable manicured lawns spread out like emerald green carpets. Farther along was the library, a glass jewel of a building, and then the back of the college, with the Cam flowing serenely by the opulent gardens. It was Prince Charles's college at Cambridge, and so they gave the code name "Trinity" to von Oberman's mission to eradicate him.

"West," Constance Higby said, "I'm going to authorize you to carry a concealed weapon. Let's make that retroactive, shall we?"

"I'm glad that somebody believes me," West said.

"It's not that I believe you, West. It's just that I don't want to look like a bloody fool if it turns out that you're right."

West nodded and began to make his exit.

"Oh, yes," she said, "Riley is now Detective Inspector. He'll be working under you."

The pipe, West thought.

"Is there something wrong with that?" Higby asked.

"Not at all, Detective Chief Inspector. That's fine with me."

They received the hand-delivered invitations on the same day.

Handwritten by Prince Charles himself, with the Prince of Wales's seal on the envelope, he was inviting his guests to spend a country weekend at Highgrove House in Gloucestershire. Those he invited were Dr. Montague Rogerson, Lady Sarah Filburn, and Prince Christian von Oberman.

Sarah phoned von Oberman.

"Did you get one?"

"Yes, I just got it. This is incredible."

"It will be fun," she said.

"What does one wear?"

"Dress for dinner," she said. "Otherwise, casual. Charles is very casual."

"Mine has a note," he said. "He wants me to look at his Earp and tell him what I think. Do I tell him the truth or do I lie?"

"I'm sure it's real. There aren't that many around. Besides, who would forge an Earp?"

"We will drive there together?"

"Of course," she said. "He expects it. The separate invitations were just a formality. You'll love the house. We're going to play tennis. How sweet."

"So you've already been there?"

"Yes," she said. "With my father. It's positively gorgeous. It's stone, with neo-classical façades, four reception rooms and six main bedrooms. And he's got stables, staff dwellings, parkland, and a home farm of nearly 350 acres. It's a tiny part of the Duchy, actually. That amounts to 126,000 acres in twenty-two counties. Most of that is on Dartmoor in Devon. The Duchy has tenant farmers, all quite medieval. The very best part of Highgrove is the new function suite Charles built in Cotswold stone. It's got a stone roof, would you believe. He calls it the Orchard Room."

"So it will be us, Charles, and, I presume, Camilla Parker-Bowles?"

"I know personally that he's also invited your shrink. Dr. Rogerson."

"He didn't mention it to me," von Oberman said.

"I expect he knows you'll be there. You still forget, Christian, that this is Britain. What's left unsaid is often more important than what is."

"I'll pick you up Friday morning?"

"The invitation says noon. Let's say ten o'clock. We're due there for lunch, so we will have time to freshen up."

"Will we share a room?"

"Does the Pope pray in the woods? Of course we'll share a room. Charles and Camilla share one. Why shouldn't we? See you Friday."

After she hung up, he took out his cell phone, punched in the numbers, and reported:

"This is Ramos. Trinity operational this weekend, Highgrove."

On Thursday night, von Oberman packed everything he would need for the weekend, including his dinner jacket, walking shoes, several shirts and sweaters, his tennis whites, and the tiny gas pistol, which he carefully placed in an undetectable compartment in his suitcase. The next morning, he picked up his yellow Porsche Boxter at the garage and drove over to Sarah's town house in Chelsea to find her waiting out front. They stuffed her bags and tennis racquet with his in the rear boot, draping his covered dinner jacket over them, and with the top down, drove off.

As they approached Tetbury, they could see Highgrove looming up in the distance, the open balustrade surmounted with urns on top of the roof. In keeping with Charles's classical tastes, he had Ionic pilasters erected in front of the house, lending it a quality of antiquity. The curved path leading to the house was lined with informal English gardens and lush trees.

Rogerson had already arrived, his Vauxhall parked below in a parking area hidden partially by trees, into which von Oberman drove his Porsche. Once inside, they were led to their room by a servile butler who carried their bags. He was, in actuality, with the Special Branch, and his function was to discreetly rummage through their belongings.

The bedroom was spacious and bright, with a four-poster bed and a fireplace, but with no bath. For that, they would be obliged to go down the hall. A portrait of Melbourne hung over the bed and another of Wellington on one of the walls. A small watercolor by Charles was hung next to it, a bucolic scene of a small stone bridge with a brook running beneath it. The butler placed their bags at the foot of the bed and hung von Oberman's dinner jacket in a closet. He bowed slightly and exited.

Von Oberman was not in the least fooled. As soon as Sarah had vanished into the bathroom, he changed and put the gas pistol in a pocket inside his jacket, where it was completely concealed. She returned wrapped in a towel and threw on a casual brown dress. It was almost noon as they descended the staircase, to be ushered into a dining room by another butler. Rogerson was already seated at the table and rose to greet them. At the very moment he stood, Charles and Camilla entered the room. He was wearing the country uniform, a houndstooth jacket, cavalry twill trousers and a grey turtle-neck, she tan slacks and a green cashmere crewneck sweater. They were both smiling amiably.

"Charles, darling," Sarah kissed him on the cheek, "you look smashing."

"No he doesn't," Camilla joked. "He looks a wreck. They just took his casts off and he has to hobble around with a crutch. He looks like a veteran from the Boer War. The leg is still all taped up and he can barely move his arm. But he's determined to play tennis."

"It's not my good arm," Charles said. "I can manage to toss the ball with the bad one and still serve properly. But it's true, running will be a problem. You will quite simply have to hit the ball directly at me."

"I will run you until you drop," Sarah laughed. "Dr. Rogerson, how are you?"

Rogerson looked lost. He was the only man wearing a necktie and seemed stiff.

"I'm quite well, actually. If His Royal Highness can't play, I can substitute for him."

"Jolly good idea," Charles said. "I will referee."

"And you will cheat," Camilla said.

I positively will not," Charles said. "The Prince of Wales does not cheat."

Charles walked uneasily over to von Oberman. It was the first time that they were actually face-to-face.

"How kind of you to come," Charles extended his hand, "and how lucky you are to have Sarah."

"Your Royal Highness, this is a great honor," von Oberman bowed slightly.

"Whatever it is, I think it's time for lunch, what?" Charles said.

He gestured for them to sit. Lunch was trout, lightly sautéed, served with a chilled Hocheimer Kirchnstruck Riesling Spatlese 1998, a full-flavored Rhine wine that was slightly too dominant for the fish, yet pleasant. Charles and Camilla presided over lunch, masterfully engaging each guest in conversation and bantering with each other across the table. Von Oberman sized up the prince. He would have to get him alone somewhere, not an easy task considering the enormous staff and the presence of the other guests. The planned activities would not make matters easier, either.

"I'm sure you appreciate that the vegetables you are eating were organically grown on the Duchy Home farm. We use absolutely no artificial pesticides and fertilizers," Charles said. "I don't suggest that all farmers go organic, but I am convinced that organic farming was, and still is, the most effective system of applying what I think to be the principles of sustainable agriculture. I have put my heart and soul into Highgrove. All the things I have tried to do in this small corner of Gloucestershire have been the physical expression of a personal philosophy."

Camilla beamed.

"Charles is still terribly surprised that so many farmers still regard organic farming as some kind of drop-out option for superannuated hippies."

Von Oberman pretended to be engrossed. Maybe he could get Charles alone on a tour of the farm.

"You must be absolutely against genetically modified crops," he said.

"Yes, precisely, and I can see that you share my sentiments. When we have a look around the farm, I will explain what I mean further. But if we can't stop it totally, at least there should be accurate labeling of ingredients produced by genetic modification. Otherwise, one has removed a fundamental choice about the food we eat. We simply do not know the long-term consequences of releasing plants bred in this way. If something does go badly wrong, we will be faced with clearing up a kind of pollution which is actually self-perpetuating."

Camilla nodded in agreement.

"Charles believes, and so do I, that this kind of genetic modification takes mankind into realms that belong to God, and to God alone."

"I can't wait to see what you've done," von Oberman said.

"So you shall, but only history will judge if I took the right decision."

"Charles, you're not still selling the books?" Sarah laughed, looking over at a table with several volumes scattered on top of it.

"Well, yes, of course. *Highgrove: Portrait of an Estate,* by Charles Clover and me, is very informative. I would give it away, but the proceeds go to The Prince's Trust to help disadvantaged children, particularly to encourage organic farming in underdeveloped countries by the impoverished. Unless we put an end to poverty, there will be no end to the population explosion. The environmental consequences will be devastating. The proceeds from *A Vision of Britain,* my book based on my BBC documentary on the destruction of the country by modern architecture, go to The Prince of Wales's Institute of Architecture through The Prince's Foundation, which brings together The School for Architecture and the Building Arts, the Urban Villages Forum, Regeneration Through Heritage, and The Phoenix Trust. No, I simply can't give them away. Every penny counts."

"Well, of course, we'll all have to buy them, won't we, Christian," Sarah said.

"You can put me down," Rogerson said.

"Splendid," Camilla said, "Now, we can all go for a walk."

Charles and von Oberman walked ahead of the others.

"Your Royal Highness," Charles addressed him. "You are a prince, aren't you?"

"Actually, yes. I am the Prince of Bavaria."

"What a pity," Charles said. "Such a noble family. Anyway, Rogerson tells me that you're the leading expert on St. John Earp."

"That's probably true, Your Royal Highness. It's wonderful that you've taken an interest."

"Well, I've got one. At least I think so. I borrowed it and jumped the gun and bought it. I'd like you to have a look at it."

"Any time you wish."

"After dinner?"

"Certainly."

Von Oberman was looking for an opening.

"What is that spectacular cerise-colored shrub? That one over there in the distance?"

Von Oberman pointed to his far left. It was several hundred yards away.

"It is lovely, isn't it," Charles said. "It's 'Cynthia.' We must have a look."

"What do you mean 'Cynthia?'"

"Rhododendron 'Cynthia,'" Charles laughed.

"You are so witty, Your Royal Highness," von Oberman said.

They left the path, leaving the others behind, and walked

in the direction of the shrub, Charles limping with his crutch. Finally trudging up to their destination, Charles sighed in admiration:

"Ah, here we are. It is positively exquisite, isn't it?"

Von Oberman looked around. They were alone. He reached inside for the gas pistol. In a moment, Charles would be dead from an apparent heart attack. All he would have to do after shooting him was to toss the pistol into a nearby pond. It would sink to the bottom and be covered with sludge. Charles suddenly vanished. Von Oberman saw movement under the shrub, where Charles, with another man, was engaged in pruning the lower branches.

"What luck," Charles shouted up at him. "If you hadn't wanted to see 'Cynthia,' my gardener would have neglected to rid the shrub of these dead branches."

The green attire of the gardener had camouflaged him as he lay under the bottom thicket of the rhododendron.

"Your Royal Highness is absolutely right," the gardener declared. "I don't know how I missed these. They didn't look so bad to me, but on close inspection, I can see where I was wrong."

Spying von Oberman, the gardener lifted himself up to his full height and extended a rough and dirty hand.

"I'm Steven, Steven MacDonald. Have you ever seen anything as beautiful as 'Cynthia' here?

"Not in a plant, I confess," von Oberman said.

"It was a gift from an American friend, Mrs. Clinton, I believe. His Royal Highness is a first-rate gardener," MacDonald said. "He keeps us on our toes, he does."

"Very good, Steven," Charles said, "I think we've got it right now."

"Thank you, sir. If you don't mind, I'll be seeing to the *Cedrus libani*."

He looked at von Oberman: "Cedar of Lebanon, sir. A true aristocrat of the tree world, and very appropriate for its owner, I would say."

MacDonald bowed subserviently and took his leave.

"This place is crawling with Special Branch," von Oberman said to himself.

All the obsequious fawning was beginning to get on von Oberman's nerves. He had taken a genuine dislike to Charles, who struck him as superficial and disingenuous. If he cared so much about poverty, why didn't he just give away his vast wealth? But perhaps it was jealousy. It would have pleased von Oberman to be real royalty, with all the trappings. In any event, there was still the job to be done. He could try again when he and Charles looked at the Earp, if indeed they did so alone. He knew he would have to be extremely cautious. It was a very English quality to place people under surveillance without their having the slightest idea they were being watched. No one was better at that. Charles enjoyed the illusion of complete freedom but his every movement was monitored, except when he was on a horse, which was why he refused to give up polo with its intrinsic dangers.

"I think it's high time we caught up with the others." Charles picked up his crutch. "And I fully intend to ignore doctor's orders and throw this away when we play tennis tomorrow."

Camilla was waving at them from a distance. "Where on earth have you been?"

"We went to visit Cynthia," Charles said. "Christian wanted to see her."

How utterly charming," said Camilla. "Are you a horticulturalist?"

"Not really. My mother's estate is exquisitely landscaped, but nothing like this."

"I should love to see it," Charles said.

"You should visit Germany soon. We love English royalty. We feel very close because you are German."

Charles clammed up and kept walking.

"Did I offend him?" von Oberman asked Camilla.

"Not at all. He's just lost in his thoughts. It will be fine."

That evening, they all descended for dinner in evening clothes. Charles wore a red sash with the seal of the Prince of Wales. As they stood around sipping sherry before dinner, a black clergyman materialized to join them.

"This is The Reverend Ansley Scott," Charles introduced him. "He will be conducting mass on Sunday at the chapel."

Scott was about sixty and had curly black hair with specks with grey. An Anglican priest, he wore the traditional black suit and clerical collar.

"I have been discussing with Father Scott how we need to rediscover the sense of the sacred in the western world. My belief is that in each one of us there is a distant echo of the sense of the sacred, but that the majority of us are terrified to admit its existence for fear of ridicule and abuse."

"That is very profound, Your Royal Highness," Scott agreed.

"You see, Father Scott, this fear of ridicule, even to the extent of mentioning the name of God, is a classic indication of the loss of meaning in so-called Western civilization."

As they proceeded to dinner, Charles continued his rambling discourse, turning on globalization as a threat to the sanctity of life on the planet.

"And that is what I fear about the whole concept of 'globalization,'" he went on, as he took his place at the head of the table. "I simply do not believe the assurances of those who tell us that the forces it unleashed can all be constrained within a framework of proper regulation."

The clergyman sat directly to Charles's right, Sarah to his left. Rogerson sat next to Sarah and von Oberman next to the clergyman. Camilla sat at the far end of the table from Charles, as she had at lunch. Listening to Charles's tirade against globalization, Rogerson became more fully aware of Harrington's motives. It was globalization that was making him even richer. But what did Charles care about making money? He had all the money he would ever need and more. It wasn't so much that he was an enlightened progressive. It was really that he had a medieval frame of mind.

Upon Charles's signal, Father Scott said grace. Dinner was lavish. Poached wild Scottish salmon was served with a Fieuzal Blanc '95.

"Superb," Rogerson managed.

"We rather prefer a Grave with salmon," Camilla said. "The bouquet is intense and it's redolent with fruit."

"Next, someone will surely note the melon and apple flavors," Sarah laughed, "with the butter, honey, and wild flowers thrown in for good measure."

Camilla winced, but Charles smiled. "I enjoy irreverence," he said. "It cuts the ice, don't you think?"

With that, the waiters cleared the table and produced pigeon with Malaysian spices on a bed of puréed leeks, served with a '97 L'Evangile Pomorol.

Following a *reine de saba,* the waiters poured champagne and Charles addressed his black guest:

"In saluting Father Ansley Scott, let me say how much pleasure the whole idea of diversity gives me. All the people from diverse backgrounds, black, brown, yellow, and the like, represent an amazing and very jolly cross section of the different communities that make up Britain. In my view, this should be a source of pride, not envy or resentment. I fully understand the problems and difficulties experienced by immigrant communities in Great Britain. What we need, I think, is a level of civilized tolerance in a multi-racial society."

"He's got it all wrong," Rogerson thought. "Britain is a white country. A few immigrants are O.K., but not a flood." To Rogerson, homogeneity was the basis of sanity and always would be. He reckoned that multiculturalism was no problem for the Prince, because all he had to do was go out in a dragon boat with a bunch of Bangladeshi in Docklands in East London, beat on a drum with a black woman in an African costume in Brixton, and then go home to St. James's Palace, or better still, drive out to Highgrove. Harrington was right, he mused. It was too bad they had called off the assassination, or so he thought. He looked over at von Oberman, who showed no sign of emotion.

Father Scott looked around the table. "This has been a very pleasant evening for me. Thank you all for being so gracious."

Charles escorted him out and then returned to the table.

"If Prince von Oberman would be so kind, I would like to show him my Earp. Of course, everybody can see it, too, but after he has had a chance to evaluate it. Camilla loves it, as do I. I certainly hope it's real."

Charles and von Oberman adjourned to the study, where the painting was hung over the fireplace. It was entitled "Rabbit at the End" and pictured a gigantic, troubled-looking blue rabbit sitting amidst what looked like the rubble following an ecological disaster of some sort. In the right-hand corner, a dwarf in a jester's cap was juggling red balls.

"From whom did you acquire this painting?" von Oberman asked.

"The collector, Sir Reginald Finkelstein."

"He has impeccable taste. Why would he sell it?"

Von Oberman reached for the pistol.

"Your port, Your Royal Highness," a butler said, carrying a silver tray with a bottle of Quinta Da Noval 1963 and two port glasses.

Von Oberman eased his hand out of his pocket and reached for a glass after Charles had taken his.

"You can put the bottle there," he instructed, pointing to a table. "He sold it to me because I asked him to."

"May I ask what you paid?"

"Of course. Fifty thousand pounds."

Good news for Sarah, von Oberman thought. This would be the base price for an Earp at the gallery. Von Oberman scrutinized the painting, touching the canvas lightly. He paused for about a minute and said, "It is authentic."

"How can you tell?"

"It's the texture of the paint. No other artist could duplicate it. His technique was unique."

Charles picked up the bottle himself and refilled their glasses.

"This is the best port in the world, a noble port," he said. "1963 was unequaled. They sold it at the buttery at my college for three pounds ten a bottle. Today, it sells for two hundred pounds a bottle."

"You were at Trinity."

"Yes, Trinity. We should let the others join us. Gladwell, another bottle and three more glasses, if you would be so kind. I think it's terribly stupid to make the women go to a separate room while the men drink port and smoke cigars, don't you think? There are some traditions that simply must go."

Rogerson examined the painting, nodding approvingly.

"Your Royal Highness, as you have suggested, there is going to be an exhibit of Earps at the Fitzwilliam Museum in Cambridge," he said. "I'm reluctant to ask, but would you honor us with your presence?"

Charles agreed. He would give a talk. He liked giving speeches on a wide range of topics and listed them all on his web site. A talk on art and its meaning, with Earp as the focal point, would do nicely.

"Unfortunately, Sarah and I will not be there, Your Royal Highness," von Oberman apologized. "She has to be in New York for the opening of her gallery, and I am giving a lecture in Germany. But I have arranged for another speaker, Professor Corine Ourschlott of Leyden University in the Netherlands. I think you will find that she will be very informative."

Rogerson looked surprised. "What a pity," he said.

"It is," von Oberman agreed. "Any occasion with His Royal Highness is one not to be missed."

"You know this Ourschlott person?" Rogerson asked.

"Of course," von Oberman said. "She is an excellent scholar and a good friend. But she can be a bit difficult to understand. Her Dutch accent is terrible."

Rogerson was startled the next morning when a butler entered his room carrying a silver cup on a tray. He was still in bed.

After a long pause, the butler said, "Temperature of your bath, Dr. Rogerson."

They followed the wonderful buffet-style English breakfast with a ludicrously anti-climactic tennis game on Charles's grass court. At first, he played with Sarah against von Oberman and Camilla and hobbled about pathetically. When he slipped and fell, everyone laughed and Charles agreed his time had come to referee and let Rogerson take his place. Everyone got slightly drunk on Pimms Cups, had lunch, took naps and then went through another lavish dinner. Von Oberman decided there was too great a risk to try again. He had changed strategies.

On Sunday, after they had all prayed under Father Scott's guidance, Charles and Camilla saw them to their cars. Rogerson, who managed a cursory expression of deference, drove off perfunctorily, leaving von Oberman and Sarah to do the sycophantic scraping. Sarah curtsied and von Oberman bowed, they tucked their books under their arms, and watched a servant pack up their belongings in the boot.

"Christian," Charles said, "if I may call you by your Christian name, it was perfectly splendid to meet you."

"My feelings exactly, Your Royal Highness."

"Charles, please."

"Charles, it has been a pleasure. And Camilla, a pleasure," von Oberman said.

Sarah gave Charles and Camilla a friendly peck and they tore off in the yellow Porsche.

"What a strange man," von Oberman observed.

"It takes one to know one," Sarah replied. "Charles bores you. There was a moment when I thought you could kill him."

"That's an exaggeration," he said.

The wind blew through Sarah's hair.

"Let's hope so," she said.

Looking as inconspicuous and nondescript as possible, von Oberman traveled by rail and bus to Scrabster in Caithness in the north of Scotland and by ferry to the Orkney Islands. It took two hours on the ferry, crossing the Pentland Firth and passing the Old Man of Hoy. He disembarked at the largest of the islands, called the Mainland, and took a taxi to the Ayre Hotel on Ayre Road in Kirkwall on the harbor front, signing in under the assumed name of James Pratt Sinclair.

"Sinclair, aye," the clerk noted in his strange Orkney accent, which was a mixture of Scottish and the verbal remnants of the islands' Nordic past that was barely comprehensible. "Ye related to the Sinclair Earls? They rebelled against King James IV, and so the castle was destroyed."

"I'm a distant relation," von Oberman lied.

"Well, let bygones be bygones," the clerk joked. "Ye here on holiday?"

"I am," von Oberman said.

"Well, you're in luck. There's gonna be a 'Bà' game. They usually happen only on Christmas Day and New Year's Day. But the Viscount Harrington has taken an interest in the game and has arranged for a special one. It breaks tradition but it could bring in tourists. The local businesses don't like it, though, there's so much damage."

"Bà" game was a corruption of "ball game," since it was played with a heavy, hard leather, cork-filled ball by competing sides of hundreds of men called the Doonies and the Uppies. Along Kirkwall's winding main street, householders and shopkeepers erected barricades across their doors and windows to insulate themselves from the impending violent clashes that inevitably erupted as each side attempted to score. A goal was scored by the Uppies if one of them was able to touch the "Bà" against a wall in the south end of the town. A Doonie had to get the "Bà" into the water of the harbor to the north, near the hotel in which von Oberman was staying.

Von Oberman had to wait two days before his meeting with the man who would give him the bomb. It was also the day of the "Bà" game. He was to go to the main street and find something called "the big tree," where the man would be waiting for him. All they had told von Oberman was that the bomb maker was an Orkney secessionist and was tall, thin, and bald. Until then, von Oberman either remained in his room, which had a view of the sea, or took short strolls by the harbor, pretending to watch the boats. By the end of the second day, the rain, which had begun as a light drizzle, had become a torrent. He had a drink at the bar and dinner in the restaurant, and returned to his room. His rendezvous was at one o'clock in the afternoon, the very time when the "Bà" game would begin. In the pandemonium, no one would notice the transaction and he would be able to depart undetected.

The next day, wearing a navy blue melton wool G-9 and a long-brim olive and rust windowpane wool cap, von Oberman headed for the historic Kirkwall downtown in the driving rain. He was carrying a dark brown leather satchel. St. Magnus Cathedral towered above the grey, squat buildings that stood in bunches in its shadow like misshapen dwarfs along the slippery and intimidating narrow flagstone streets. Broad Street snaked its way from north to south, the spectators huddled under umbrellas to protect themselves from the downpour.

Von Oberman spied a small boy running toward him.

"Where is 'The Big Tree?'" he asked.

"Doon the toon," the boy shouted and pointed.

Directly in the middle of the road at the southern end of the street, as if sprouting from the flagstone, a large tree stood. Standing beside it was a tall, gaunt man, almost completely bald except for some white strands of hair that shot out wildly from the sides of his head. He was holding something.

At precisely one o'clock, someone threw the "Bà" from the "Mercat Cross" into the crowd of men in front of the cathedral. Players formed a tight scrum around it, while others braced themselves against the buildings to prevent opposing players from gaining ground.

Von Oberman approached the man, who handed him the grey Mac Power Book.

"What is this?" a startled von Oberman asked.

"It's the bomb," the man whispered. "It's in the computer. You must punch in the day, date, and exact time you want it to go off. Then, press enter."

The thundering mob behind von Oberman roared down the side streets, kicking and tossing the "Bà" back and forth as the men shouted and pushed each other. Some climbed to the rooftops, madly running, then descending to quickly form a scrum again.

"Run," the man said. "And don't forget to recharge the battery."

The man fled down a dark, narrow alley. Von Oberman unzipped the satchel and put the computer in it. Then he tore up the street towards the harbor, the rain pelting against his face almost like sleet. He caught sight of the P&O ferry preparing to depart, the loud blast of its horn chilling him to his core. Suddenly he found himself surrounded by furious players sweeping him along towards the water. Von Oberman was desperate. He held the satchel high in the air, unable to break free. As they reached the water's edge, a craggy, drenched old man in a kilt, who was fiercely holding onto the "Bà," dumped it into the water to the deafening cheers of his teammates. It was Viscount Harrington. He and von Oberman were face to face, the Viscount grinning and chattering wildly, like an ape. Someone on the ferry's deck caught sight of Harrington signaling for it to wait.

"Go," he ordered von Oberman, who ran to the ferry, jumping aboard as it pulled away.

Stanley West saw the article immediately. It was front-page news. Prince Charles was to open the St. John Earp exhibit to be held at the Fitzwilliam Museum in Cambridge. The Honorary Chairman of the St. John Earp Society, "Dr. Montague Rogerson" would introduce the Prince of Wales, who was to "give a speech on art and its meaning in today's Britain." Following the Prince's speech, "Professor Doctor Corine Ourschlott of Leyden University, a noted Earp authority," as she was described in the article, "will speak on Earp's work, and particularly the painting 'Rabbit at the End,' which His Royal Highness has so graciously lent to the exhibition." A champagne reception was to follow.

West took out the first article about Earp and Rogerson from the top drawer of his desk and compared the two. He showed them both to Joe Riley.

"What do you notice?" he asked.

"What do you mean?"

"There's something in the first that isn't in the second."

Riley looked more carefully.

"I can't say that I notice anything significant."

"Look again."

Riley read both articles yet again.

"It sounds like a bunch of hype to me. I don't understand modern art. Never have. And I've never set foot in the Fitzbilly. It sounds like just another excuse for Chuck to sound off about something he knows nothing about. I'd pay for the Queen but not for the rest of them. I think His Royal Highness should get a job, maybe with the phone company. Or with the post office. Something useful, you know."

"No. No. That's not it. The German art expert Prince Christian von Oberman is mentioned prominently in the first article, but not at all in the second. To me, that's the sound of the dog not barking."

What does *The Hound of the Baskervilles* have to do with this?" Riley asked.

"It's not *The Hound of the Baskervilles*. It's *The Tale of the Silver Blaze*. Why would Prince von Oberman miss an event like that? And if Michael Rogerson were involved in an attempt on the Prince's life, perhaps his brother is connected in some way. I believe we should attend."

"If we must, but unless you're right, which I strongly doubt, it'll bore me to tears," Riley said. "Do we go as guests or as police?"

"Both," West said.

A crowd gathered outside the Fitzwilliam on the evening of the opening of the exhibition to catch a glimpse of Prince Charles. He emerged in immaculately tailored evening dress from the royal Rolls, looking dashing, and waving amiably. Apart from a slight limp, His Royal Highness appeared to be jaunty. He entered the museum followed by a contingent from the Special Branch.

About a hundred men and women in evening clothes stood about in the Adeane Gallery, which had been converted into a gallery for the arts in the twentieth century. A large group was focusing on "Rabbit at the End," which the curator, Julian Avery, had hung prominently by itself in a place of honor. Charles then entered the gallery. He made his way through the crowd of guests, shaking hands, as each guest bowed or curtsied politely to him.

"Jolly good show," a middle-aged woman with silver hair joked.

"Indeed," Charles grinned, as he made his way to the podium.

"Ladies and gentleman, please take your seats," Julian Avery instructed.

West and Riley, both in dinner jackets, sat in the last row, West on the aisle and Riley in the seat next to him. Seated at the podium with Prince Charles were Dr. Montague Rogerson, Julian Avery and a middle-aged woman with mousy hair in a bun. She was wearing a modest black evening dress and her features were nondescript, except that she had a slightly bulbous nose. Her rimless spectacles gave her an austere and academic demeanor. At her feet was a dark brown leather satchel, which had been opened and searched by a Special Branch officer, who found nothing but running clothes and a Mac Power Book, which she explained she would be using during her lecture. He had flipped open the computer, closed it, and handed it back to her. She sat directly to Charles's right, with Rogerson to his left.

Julian Avery, a smarmy and unctuous man of about thirty, walked to the lectern and tapped the microphone to get the attention of the audience. Totally self-absorbed and filled with the self-importance of someone of note in the arts world, Avery basked in the presence of his illustrious guest. There was no degree of sycophancy of which he was incapable in the promotion of his own notoriety.

"It is an extraordinary honor for us and for the Fitzwilliam Museum that His Royal Highness has not only graced us with his presence at the opening of the St. John Earp exhibition. He has also contributed bountifully to the success of this landmark event by lending to the exhibition his superb Earp, 'Rabbit at the End.' "

The audience applauded mightily.

"You haven't come here to listen to me, although I will take a moment to note the growing recognition of the work of Jim Earp. His Royal Highness has contributed in no small measure to this phenomenon as a patron of the St. John Earp Society. He has, with his intelligence and insight, energized us all. And here to introduce him to us is the honorary chairman of the St. John Earp Society, Dr. Montague Rogerson."

Rogerson rose to polite applause. His short speech, which he had reduced to a few notes that he had scribbled on a small pad, managed to have little or no content. He thanked the Prince for his patronage and said he was looking forward to his remarks, "which no, doubt, will enlighten us, not only on the significance of Earp but of the role of the arts in Britain today. Indeed that is the title of his speech. Following his speech, we will hear an important lecture by our distinguished visiting scholar from The Netherlands, Professor Doctor Corine Ourschlott of Leyden University."

The Special Branch had confirmed some weeks before that there was a Professor Corine Ourschlott at Leyden University, but that she was traveling in Estonia and could not be reached.

"Please join me in giving His Royal Highness Prince Charles a most warm and deserving welcome."

Charles walked slowly to the podium and took his notes from his inside jacket pocket, laying them before him. He began to speak.

"Speaking on the subject of the role of the arts in Britain today is a daunting task. Oscar Wilde said that the arts had no use and that their sole function was to provide us with pleasure. In all due respect to one of the greatest playwrights in the English language, who was also an exquisite poet and novelist, I am not convinced that Wilde really meant this entirely. Certainly, *The Picture of Dorian Gray* is a highly moral work, condemning the self-absorption and selfishness that can be a corrupting influence in any society. Moreover, Wilde's essay, "The Spirit of Man Under Socialism," shows us that the great playwright understood the relationship between the arts and the well-being of his fellow man.

"The same is true of the great Greek playwright, Aristophanes, whose comic play, *The Frogs,* was written to illustrate his point that the greatest artists are the ones who teach us to be better citizens. For this reason, Dionysus judges Aeschylus to be the greatest playwright, and not Euripides. For the same reasons, were I to judge amongst the British artists, I would place St. John Earp at the top. His moral instruction, be it against nuclear war, the decline of British cultural vitality, and the ecological recklessness that threatens our planet, behooves us to place him above those artists who simply seek to provide us with an aesthetic lollipop or a momentary shock to the senses. The very painting that I have lent to the exhibit, 'Rabbit at the End,' is illustrative of precisely this point."

After rambling on in the same vein, Charles closed by exhorting the audience to view the Earps on exhibit "in the spirit of a new commitment to the arts in Britain as a force for a cultural renaissance to rival that of the English Renaissance of Queen Elizabeth I. It behooves us all to recall Wilde's words from *De Profundis:* 'He is the Philistine who upholds and aids the heavy, cumbrous, blind, mechanical forces of society, and who does not recognize dynamic force when he meets it either in man or a movement.'"

As Charles gathered up his papers, the audience rose in appreciation with sustained applause. He nodded back, and returned to his seat, making a few discreet remarks to Rogerson and then to Ourschlott. Julian Avery returned to the podium to thank the Prince and to introduce the guest lecturer, "whose talk is entitled 'Painting As Narrative; A Repudiation of Clement Greenberg.'"

No sooner had Ourschlott begun droning, looking down from time to time at her computer to consult her notes, various texts, or images of paintings, than the audience began to drift off. Charles looked upward and stifled a yawn. West noticed a Special Branch officer beginning to dose off. She mercifully concluded by referring to "Rabbit at the End," which she pointed to as she spoke.

"This incredible painting," she said in her thick Dutch accent, "shows conclusively that narrative in art is not only possible but essential. This is an exquisite composition in and of itself, but it also challenges us to perceive the world in a new way, which, in the end, is the function of the imagination."

Julian Avery rushed over to the podium to shake hands with Ourschlott and thank her. The exhausted audience showed its appreciation with light clapping, as Avery invited everyone to join His Royal Highness for the champagne reception. Charles and the others on the podium came down to the floor as the guests milled about, examining the paintings and fawning over the Prince. Ourschlott, before coming down, typed a few keys and closed her computer, carrying it and the satchel down with her. She placed the Power Book in a corner of the gallery and excused herself, asking for the location of the W.C. A guard pointed in its direction and she walked out of the gallery towards it, carrying the satchel.

When she failed to appear after about five minutes, West, who had noticed her actions, looked around the gallery until his eyes fell on the Power Book.

"I don't like the looks of that," he said to Riley, who was guzzling a glass of champagne.

"Of what?"

"That Power Book," he said, suddenly bolting towards it and picking it up. He held it to his ear. He could hear the quiet ticking.

"Follow me," he said to Riley and rushed to an exit, opening the door and shouting, "Run for cover," as he tossed the computer out into the street.

A Special Branch officer grabbed him.

"What on earth are you doing?" he asked, just as the bomb exploded outside. It would have killed everyone in the gallery.

"What in God's name was that?" the Special Branch officer shouted, as they whisked Charles out of the gallery. The guests, in a state of panic, began pushing to get out.

West broke free from the Special Branch officer's grasp and ran outside, Riley following him. Beyond the debris, West saw a figure running in the dark. He pulled out a torch and shined it on the runner, as he shouted, "You, wait. Stop."

The figure kept running. West could see her in the beam of his torch. She was tall, dark, and stunning, in running shorts and a T-shirt, and was wearing a knapsack. West ordered Riley to go after her. A strong runner, Riley soon was directly behind her, yelling at her to stop. She turned, looked straight at him, and fired her tiny pistol, the bullet entering his skull through his forehead. As Riley fell, he provided West, who had just caught up to them, with a shield. He fired three bullets into the runner before she could get off another shot and she fell backwards, dislodging her black wig as her head hit the ground. West bent over the body and removed the wig to see von Oberman's close-cropped blond hair beneath it.

"The Prince is dead," he said.

Epilogue

West was leaving work early to take Margaret to the marathon Last Night at the Proms at Albert Hall. He stuck his head into Constance Higby's office to tell her he was going.

"Did you hear about Michael Rogerson?" she asked. "It just came over the wireless."

"No," West said.

"The circus brought in a sick lion to be treated," she related. "Rogerson anaesthetized it. He needed to take out its appendix. He got it on the operating table and thought he had put it to sleep, but it woke up and bit his head off."

"You're joking," West said.

"No, it's the truth, really."

West shook his head in disbelief. He went to fetch Margaret and they took the train to London. They sat quietly until Margaret began to speak:

"Stanley, I was going over our accounts and we're short a thousand pounds."

West sighed. "I have something to confess. I lost it in a poker game with some Americans at that British-American police conference in Brighton. It was stupid. I was going to tell you, but I couldn't get myself to do it."

"Oh, Stanley, what a waste. It would have paid for a fortnight in Italy."

"Well," West said, "I'm a Detective Superintendent now. I'll make it up."

"Just don't ever do it again," Margaret said.

"You don't have to worry about that, dear."

"Anyway, I think the Queen should give you the Order of the British Empire, the OBE, for what you did. You saved Charles's life."

"It was just in the line of duty," West said. "Riley died, which is more than I did."

Albert Hall was resplendent. People wore party hats and waved Union Jacks and the banner of St. George during the sing-along of British patriotic songs. West and Margaret stood high up in a balcony, holding hands, singing "Rule Britannia!" at the top of their lungs.

"Stanley," Margaret said, "It's wonderful to be English."

West was silent.

"Don't you think so?" Margaret asked.

"I do," West said. "That's not it. I don't know why I did not think of this before."

"What didn't you think of? You think of everything, Stanley."

"Viscount 'Arrington. Michael Rogerson was his vet."

"You mean ..."

West smiled.

IF YOU LIKED THIS BOOK, YOU WON'T WANT TO MISS OTHER TITLES BY DANDELION BOOKS!

Available Now And Always Through www.GoOff.com
And Affiliated Websites.

Fiction:

Adventure Capital, by John Rushing...South Florida adventure, crime and violence in a fiction story based on a true life experience. A book you will not want to put down until you reach the last page. (ISBN 1893302083)

Freedom Beyond Ground Zero: Letting Go of Anxiety, Grief and Fear of the Unknown, by Jim Britt... Jeremy Carter, a fireman from Missouri who is in New York City for the day, decides to take a tour of the Trade Center, only to watch in shock, the attack on its twin towers from a block away. Afterward as he gazes at the pit of rubble and talks with many of the survivors, Jeremy starts to explore the inner depths of his soul, to ask questions he'd never asked before. This dialogue helps him learn who he is and what it takes to overcome the fear, anger, grief and anxiety this kind of tragedy brings. (ISBN 1893302741)

Return To Masada, by Robert G. Makin... In a gripping account of the famous Battle of Masada, Robert G. Makin skillfully recaptures the blood and gore as well as the spiritual essence of this historic struggle for freedom and independence. (ISBN 1893302105)

Unfinished Business, by Elizabeth Lucas Taylor... Lindsay Mayer knows something is amiss when her husband, Griffin, a college professor, starts spending too much time at his office and out-of-town. Shortly after the ugly truth surfaces, Griffin disappears altogether. Lindsay is shattered. Life without Griffin is life without life... One of the sexiest books you'll ever read! (ISBN 1893302687)

The Woman With Qualities, by Sarah Daniels... South Florida isn't exactly the Promised Land that forty-nine-year-old newly widowed Keri Anders had in mind when she transplanted herself here from the northeast... A tough action-packed novel that is far more than a love story. (ISBN 1893302113)

Diving Through Clouds, by Nicola Lindsay... Kate is dying...dying...dead; but not quite. Total demise would have deprived her guardian angel, Thomas, from taking her on a nose-dive through the clouds of self-denial to see herself in the eyes of the friends and family she left behind. A spiritual journey from a gifted fiction writer. (ISBN 1893302199)

Non-Fiction:

America, Awake! We Must Take Back Our Country, by Norman Livergood... This book is intended as a wake-up call for Americans, as Paul Revere awakened the Lexington patriots to the British attack on April 18, 1775, and as Thomas Paine's *Common Sense* roused apathetic American colonists to recognize and struggle against British oppression. Our current situation is similar to that which American patriots faced in the 1770s: a country ruled by "foreign" and "domestic" plutocratic powers and a divided citizenry uncertain of their vital interests. (ISBN 189330227X)

The New World Order Exposed: How A Cabal of International Bankers Is Deliberately Trying To Undermine America, by Victor Thorn... "Yes, Virginia, there is a New World Order," writes Victor Thorn in this gutsy, impassioned, no-holds-barred book about The Controllers' global plot to undermine America. Who are the Controllers? You will learn about this cabal of international bankers that controls the Federal Reserve System and is responsible for creating a New World Order with an agenda to strip Americans of their rights and make the country into a military dictatorship. (ISBN 1893302717)

Seeds Of Fire: China And The Story Behind The Attack On America, by Gordon Thomas... The inside story about China that no one can afford to ignore. Using his unsurpassed contacts in Israel, Washington, London and Europe, Gordon Thomas, internationally acclaimed best-selling author and investigative reporter for over a quarter-century, reveals information about China's intentions to use the current crisis to launch itself as a new Super-Power and become America's new major enemy... *"This has been kept out of the news agenda because it does not suit certain business interests to have that truth emerge...Every patriotic American should buy and read this book... it is simply revelatory* (Ray Flynn, Former U.S. Ambassador to the Vatican.) (ISBN 1893302547)

The Last Atlantis Book You'll Ever Have To Read! by Gene D. Matlock... More than 25,000 books, plus countless other articles have been written about a fabled confederation of city-states known as Atlantis. If it really did exist, where was it located? Does anyone have valid evidence of its existence – artifacts and other remnants? According to historian, archaeologist, educator and linguist Gene D. Matlock, both questions can easily be answered. (ISBN 1893302202)

The Last Days Of Israel, by Barry Chamish... With the Middle East crisis ongoing, *The Last Days of Israel* takes on even greater significance. Barry Chamish, investigative reporter who has the true story about Yitzak Rabin's assassination, tells it like it is. (ISBN 1893302164)

The Courage To Be Who I Am, by Mary-Margareht Rose... This book is rich with teachings and anecdotes delivered with humor and humanness, by a woman who followed her heart and learned to listen to her inner voice; in the process, transforming every obstacle into an opportunity for testing her courage to manifest her true identity. (1SBN 189330213X)

ALL DANDELION BOOKS ARE AVAILALBLE THROUGH WWW.GOOFF.COM AND AFFILIATED WEBSITES... ALWAYS.